T0158973

Home at Last
An Acadian Journey

Ollie Porche Voelker

Illustrated by Heidi Voelker and Tess Davis

Inspiring Voices®
A Service of Guideposts

Acknowledgments

Many thanks to Maurice Basque, scientific advisor at the Institute of Acadian Studies at the University of Moncton in Moncton, New Brunswick, and Michelle Johnson, curator/director of the Acadian Memorial in St. Martinville, Louisiana, who read my manuscript for historical accuracy. Thanks to the people who patiently and willingly answered my many questions—especially Chris Bonura at the Port of New Orleans; Roger Sevigny, historian at the Historic Site in Grand Pré, Nova Scotia; Rene Schmit, county agent of St. Charles Parish; and the tour guides at Destrehan Plantation. If there are any errors, they are mine. Either I misinterpreted the facts or didn't ask the right questions.

Special thanks to the members of my critique groups—Carol Ashley, Judy Creekmore, Renelle Folse, Carole Ford, Regina Gautreaux, Jodie Harris, and Candy Olson—for their friendship, help, encouragement, and careful reading of my manuscript.

Thanks to my husband, Bill, who read several drafts, and also to Marlene Walker and my former coworkers Diana Richards and Sharon Dowty, who proofread an early draft. To my daughter Heidi and granddaughter Tess who helped to make my dream come true with their illustrations.

To the faculty and staff of the Institute of Children's Literature in West Redding, Connecticut, who initially accompanied me down this path.

To my children, grandchildren, family, and friends for their support, encouragement, and belief that I could reach my goal.

And to everyone else who encouraged me along this journey.

Part One
Nova Scotia, Canada
Summer–Fall 1755

Acadie

1755

1

English Soldiers

Nova Scotia, Canada, Summer 1755

The pounding on the door grew louder and louder. Men shouted and kicked the door. I couldn't understand what they were saying, but they sounded like the sailors who often came to Grand Pré in their trading ships. My eight-year-old brother, Michel, and I jumped out of our bed in the dark loft and peered down the steps. Four soldiers in English uniforms rushed into the house with their guns drawn when *Papa* opened the door.

I couldn't breathe. I was afraid they would hear my heart pounding. Michel shivered as he pressed his body against mine. I held him close while the soldiers dashed around the room, knocking furniture over, looking under mattresses, and throwing clothes around. They found Papa's two muskets and then raced to the barn behind the house.

"Since you refuse to fight *with* us, you won't be able to fight *against* us," yelled the last soldier to leave the house, mixing enough French words with his English for us to understand him.

My poor *maman's* neat house was a mess, and we all shook with fright. My four-year-old brother, Jacques, and my little sisters, Brigette and Anne, held tightly to Maman, who stood near the fireplace. Our clean clothes were scattered everywhere. Mattresses leaned against the beds. Wherever we walked, our shoes crunched on broken dishes, and we tracked flour across the floor. Papa ran outside but hurried back carrying another gun.

"The soldiers ran toward *Grand-père's* house when they left our barn," said Papa. "Luckily, they didn't find this musket. I hid it under a floorboard in the barn so I can get to it quickly when I'm working in the fields, to protect our animals from foxes and coyotes. I planned to give this one to you, Pierre, because you've been working harder and helping more in the fields lately. But I'll have to keep it until I can get another one for myself."

Instead of going to work in the fields right after breakfast the next morning, we met our neighbors in front of the village church. People stood in small groups, talking in whispers. They kept looking around as if they were afraid of someone or something.

The men were dressed in linen shirts, knee-length pants, long socks, and straw hats. The women wore blouses and long skirts in shades of tan and brown. Bonnets covered their dark hair. The children were dressed like their parents. Everyone wore moccasins or wooden shoes.

A tall man, *M.* (Monsieur) Landry, stood on the church steps. Everyone gathered close to listen to him. "The soldiers raided all of our houses during the night and took our guns," he shouted. "A few weeks ago, they took our boats. What are we going to do about it?"

"Move away like many of our neighbors did a few years ago. They're now living peacefully in lands controlled by the French," our neighbor M. Thibodeau answered.

"But this is our land. Our people have lived here for 150 years," said Papa. "We worked hard to build our homes and farms."

"We'll meet again to decide what we will do," said M. Landry. "Go home now, think about it, and pray."

After supper the next evening, we walked through our apple orchard to Grand-père's house. Just as we arrived, an English soldier in white breeches, a bright red coat, and a three-cornered hat brought a letter from Lieutenant-Governor Charles Lawrence. "My orders are to go to every house in Grand Pré to read this letter. You'd better listen if you know what's good for you." He read in French, "Acadians who still have guns will be punished. All guns are to be brought to the village and turned over to the English soldiers."

Papa went home to get the musket that was supposed to be mine. He had taught me how to shoot two years earlier, when I was nine, but he often told me I would have to be more responsible before I could have my own gun. He always said, "Pierre, you spend too much time daydreaming and not enough time working."

When he came back with the gun, Papa said, "I'm sorry, Pierre. I'm afraid of what they will do to our family if I don't give them this gun too."

My heart sank, but I couldn't argue. One look at his face and I knew he was as upset as I was. I choked back my tears. Since he thought I was old enough to have my own gun, I couldn't let him see me cry. "Don't worry, Papa. They'll give them back soon."

"I hope you're right, Pierre."

Our neighbors turned in many more guns over the next few days.

The men in our village met to choose several people to write a letter to Lieutenant-Governor Lawrence. "Please give our guns back," they wrote. "We need them for protection from wild animals. We don't use our guns to shoot people."

Fifteen men traveled to Halifax, the capital of Nova Scotia, to meet with the lieutenant-governor. For the next few weeks, everyone in Grand Pré waited for the men to return so we could hear the lieutenant-governor's answer.

2

Trouble with the English

I stayed awake long after everyone else went to sleep that night. The only thing I could think about was the sailing ship in the harbor. I'm old enough to sail, I thought. I'm tired of working on our farm. Why shouldn't I have fun and go with Jean? I'll tell Papa tomorrow that I've made up my mind. I'm leaving.

After we finished feeding the animals and cleaning the barns the next morning, Jean and I went fishing using weirs, the way our friends the Micmac Indians taught us. We let Michel tag along to help us carry the fish home.

"How do fishing weirs work, Pierre?" asked Michel, just before we reached a shallow stream. He loved a story, even when he had heard it before.

"Look at that long row of sticks standing on end, side by side across the stream," said Jean. "Pierre and I put them there early in the spring."

"Why?" asked Michel.

"This stream runs into Minas Basin, then into the Bay of Fundy," I said. "Every day the water in the bay rises at high tide, pushing more water into the basin, then into the stream. As the water rises, it covers the sticks. Many fish swim over the sticks into the stream."

"The water runs back into the bay at low tide," continued Jean. "But it isn't deep enough for the fish to swim back over the sticks. They are caught swimming around behind the sticks, and we can easily scoop them up."

"Look at all the codfish and mackerel," shouted Michel as we filled our wooden buckets. "Fresh fish for dinner! But what are we going to do with so many?"

I picked up a heavy wooden bucket. "We'll bring some to Maman and Grand'maman."

"And to my maman," said Jean.

"We'll give the rest to the families of the men who went to Halifax to meet with the lieutenant-governor," I said. "They don't have time to go fishing."

I decided to talk to Papa about the sailing ship that afternoon after dinner. I often talked to him about my dream of being a ship's boy. But he always said, "Pierre, you're our oldest child. You know we need your help around the farm. An Acadian boy doesn't run off on a sailing ship. He helps his family until he is old enough to get married. Then he builds his own house and farms his land close to his family's home. He and his papa work together and help each other. That's the way of life for Acadians."

"That's not the kind of life I want, Papa" was my usual answer.

"We'll see when you're older, Pierre."

Papa hardly touched the delicious fresh fish, or the peas and turnips from Maman's garden, or her crusty, hot bread. He got up from the table and paced around the yard, to the barn, and around the apple orchard, smoking his pipe. His shoulders drooped, making him look like an old man. I didn't want to give him something else to worry about, so I changed my mind about talking to him. I would wait until later.

Michel and I spent the afternoon helping Papa in the wheat field. Then we picked pears for Maman and pulled the weeds in her vegetable garden. After supper we walked to Grand-père's house, stopping to ask Jean to go with us. Grand-père sat in his favorite chair in the front yard, whittling a piece of wood. He liked to make small animals for his grandchildren.

We went inside to give Grand'maman a kiss. She was cleaning the kitchen after supper.

"The fish was delicious, boys. I have a cake in the oven. We'll eat some in a few minutes."

I sniffed. "Umm, I smell pears. That means pear cake. I can hardly wait to taste it." Her cakes were even better than Maman's.

I sat on the ground near Grand-père's chair. "Grand-père, why is everyone so unhappy? What is Papa worried about? Do the English soldiers hate us enough to make us leave our homes?"

Grand-père put the wood and knife down. "The soldiers have to do what Lieutenant-Governor Lawrence tells them to do. I think he is worried because there are many more Acadians than English soldiers. The lieutenant-governor is afraid we could easily defeat his soldiers if we joined the French in a fight against the English."

"Why does he think we'd fight with the French soldiers?" I asked.

"I know. Our people came here from France," said Jean.

Grand-père nodded. "Yes. And we speak French. And we belong to the Catholic Church as most French people do. Most of the English are Protestants. We're happier with our own people."

"Why does anyone have to fight?" asked Michel. "Why can't everyone just get along?"

"The French and English haven't gotten along for many years," said Grand-père. "Over two hundred years ago, Jacques Cartier, a French explorer, claimed this land for France. Around the same time, English explorers claimed land farther south. But the English also wanted the land claimed by the French because of the abundance of fish, good shipping routes, and good harbors."

"They wanted our land?" I asked.

"Yes, this land the French named *Acadie* (Acadia). The two countries fought many times. Sometimes the French won, and they governed the people here. At other times, the English won, and they governed our people. We have been ruled by the English for the last forty-five years. They changed the name from Acadie to Nova Scotia, which mean 'New Scotland.'"

"I like the name Acadie better," I said.

"So do the other Acadians who live here. That's why *we* still call it Acadie."

"What happened after the English changed the name?" asked Jean.

"Until about five years ago," continued Grand-père, "every few years the governor asked Acadians to sign an oath, a promise, that we would be loyal to the king of England. We refused because we didn't want to fight for either country. But we were always told that if we signed, we would never have to fight against the French, and we could continue to worship God as Catholics. We were also told if we didn't sign the oath, we would have to leave Acadie. So we agreed to the oath."

"But Acadians can't write," I said. "How could they sign the oath?"

"It's true that many Acadians can't read or write. No one in our family ever learned how to sign his name. If he couldn't write, a man made a cross next to his own name, which was written by an English soldier.

"*Ecoutez! Qu'est que ca?*" (Listen! What is that?) asked Grand-père. "Someone is coming." At the sound of voices, we looked toward the woods. Then Grand-père breathed a sigh of relief. "It's just some Micmac Indians passing by."

"Time to come in," said Grand'maman. She sliced the warm cake and poured big glasses of cool milk for Jean, Michel, and me. She gave Grand-père a glass of spruce beer.

My mouth watered. I couldn't wait to taste the cake, but I remembered my manners. "*Merci* (Thank you), Grand'maman."

"*Il n'ya pas de quoi.*" (You're welcome.)

"Mmm, this cake is good," Michel murmured with his mouth full.

I ate the last delicious crumbs on my plate. "Please finish the story, Grand-père."

He drained his glass of spruce beer. "About five years ago, Edward Cornwallis was named the new governor of Nova Scotia. He demanded that we sign the oath again and promise to fight with the English, against the French, in case of war. Your papa and I joined a number of Acadians who asked permission to leave Nova Scotia. We wanted to move to another part of Canada where many French people were living in peace. The governor was afraid that would make the French people too strong, so he refused to let us leave."

"Why did you want to leave?" I asked. "This is our home."

"We're peaceful people," said Grand-père. "We're friendly with everyone. We trade with the English and the French. The Micmacs are our friends. We'd rather leave our homes than fight. For the first time, we understood that we aren't wanted here, but we won't be allowed to leave. We could have escaped through the woods at night like many Acadians did, but we didn't want to do that."

"Little Wolf told me his people are afraid the English will make them leave their land," I said.

Grand-père sighed. "Yes, the English want the land where the Micmacs live, hunt, and trap. And they're afraid the Micmacs will join us and the French, if there is any fighting here."

"Why would the Micmacs fight with us against the English?" asked Jean.

"They feel safe with us. They live in the forests. They know we don't want to cut down trees to farm the land. We prefer to farm the marshland, which is closer to the water. They also know we like to trade with them. Your papa and I often trade with Great Wolf, Little Wolf's papa."

"Little Wolf is our friend."

"Yes, he taught you how to fish and trap animals."

"Will our people ever fight?" I asked.

"No," said Grand-père. "We want to take care of our families, live peacefully, worship God, and enjoy life. We won't fight."

Grand'maman smiled at us. "You'd better go home because it will soon be dark. Since the English soldiers raided our house, I'm always worried, especially in the evening. I'm afraid because I don't know what the English will do next, and I don't feel safe anymore.

"Pierre, I'll give you a piece of cake for your papa. I know your maman doesn't feel like baking right now, with all the work she has to do, and with a new baby coming soon."

Grand-père walked to the door with us. "I'll need your help checking the dikes tomorrow morning. We can't let saltwater leak into the fields and kill our grain."

"If we come back tomorrow evening, will you tell us another story?" I asked.

"Yes, I want to tell you more about our people," said Grand-père.

Jean grinned as we kissed them both good night. "We'll be back for your stories and Grand'maman's cake."

But before Grand-père could tell us another story about the French and English, we had more important things to think about and talk about, things that would change our lives forever.

3

Bad News

The next morning, Jean, Michel, Grand-père, and I checked the dikes. Munching on juicy pears as we walked through the orchard, we passed a row of willow trees. Jean and I raced through the meadow to the marsh where our wheat grew tall and waved gently in the breeze. We climbed to the top of the dike. The wheat fields were golden in the sun. In the distance, apple, pear, and cherry orchards and vegetable gardens surrounded the houses in our village. Behind the houses was the forest. On the other side of the dike, the water in Minas Basin flowed slowly toward the Bay of Fundy. It was low tide and the trading ship swayed slightly in the water. The blue sky seemed endless. Everything looked so peaceful that I wanted the day to last forever.

I took a deep breath. The colorful wildflowers on the village side of the dike perfumed the air with a sweet fragrance. I gazed as far as I could in all directions, trying to memorize everything. I knew then that I never wanted to leave Grand Pré. But a little tightness in the middle of my chest reminded me I might not have a choice.

I shook off that feeling and ran to catch up with the others. "Please tell us about the dikes, Grand-père."

He bent over, looking for leaks. "I'll tell you the story my grand-père told me when I was a little boy. When he and my grand'maman came to Port Royal, Acadie in 1671, Acadian men were already building dikes. And we're still building them today the way our ancestors did. At low tide, they drove great logs, standing upright, side by side, into the ground. The men put others sideways next to the upright logs. Then they packed big square chunks of mud between and around the logs. They wanted the dikes to be high and wide. It was a big job, and they could only build a small part in a day."

"Why did they build dikes, Grand-père?" asked Michel.

"Before the Acadians built the dikes, when the tide rose every day in the Bay of Fundy, water was pushed into the basin, and all of this marshland was flooded. The Acadians wanted to use the land for farming. They didn't want to chop down lots of trees to use forestland for their farms because that would take away land used by the Micmacs. The only way they could farm the marshland was by building dikes to keep out the water from the Bay of Fundy."

I jumped down into a ditch that ran under the dike. "And they made the *aboiteaux*."

"Yes," said Grand-père, "the gates allow water to drain through the ditches from the land back into the basin. But the gates won't open to let salty water run from the sea to the land to destroy our crops. After building the dikes, the Acadians had to wait two or three years for rainwater to drain the salt from the land before they could plant their crops."

"They were patient, weren't they, Grand-père?" said Michel.

"They were patient and clever, and now our land is so productive that we have enough food for ourselves and plenty to send to the Acadians in Louisbourg. They don't have good land for farming."

That evening while we were eating supper, the sound of voices brought us all to the window. Papa went outside and talked to *Oncle*

(Uncle) Jules and two of our neighbors for a few minutes. Then he came back to tell us the news. "A tradesman from Halifax, M. Gray, arrived in Grand Pré with information about the men who met with Lieutenant-Governor Lawrence. He was too tired to talk, except to say we'll meet after breakfast tomorrow. I'm going to tell the other neighbors."

The next morning we rushed through our chores and a breakfast of leftover bread and milk. We were so anxious to hear what M. Gray had to say about the men and our guns that Maman didn't take time to cook. As usual, Jean and I walked to the village church together.

Jean hurried down the path. "Do you think the lieutenant-governor will give our guns and boats back to us?"

"I hope so, because then I'll have my own gun, at last," I said, thinking only about myself.

All eyes turned to M. Gray as he climbed the steps of our church. The only sound was the rustle of leaves in the trees. "I was in Halifax when Lieutenant-Governor Lawrence met with your men. They wouldn't allow me inside, but the lieutenant-governor's secretary, who is my friend, told me what happened. M. Hébert spoke for the men. He told the lieutenant-governor that Acadians need their boats for fishing, and guns for protection from wild animals. He explained that the guns wouldn't be used for fighting. The lieutenant-governor insisted that everyone had to sign the oath—but it includes a promise to fight with the English against the French. When the men refused to sign, Lieutenant-Governor Lawrence had them thrown into prison."

"What is going to happen to them?" cried *Mme* (Madame) Hébert.

M. Martin stepped to the front of the group. "What can we do to help?"

M. Gray sighed and shook his head. "I don't think you can do anything. The men will remain in prison. They'll never be allowed to come back home."

"No!" shouted one of the women as others moaned and cried.

My first thought was that our family was lucky because neither Papa nor my uncles had been chosen to go to Halifax. Then I looked around and realized that many of my friends and neighbors weren't so lucky. A great weight seemed to press down on my shoulders because of the sadness of so many people.

"What's going to happen to us?" asked a man standing in the back of the crowd. "Do you think Lieutenant-Governor Lawrence will make us leave our homes if we refuse to fight? For years we've been told if we don't sign the oath, we can't live here."

soldiers are still living there, and we can't be sure why they're in Grand Pré."

My heart sank. "What's going to happen, Papa?"

"I don't know, son, but I don't like it."

Instead of going back to work, Papa went to see Grand-père and Oncle Jules. Before that week, he never spent time talking during the day. There was always work to be done—feeding the animals, cleaning the barn, working on the dikes, working in the fields. And our wheat was ready to be harvested.

"Let's go fishing," said Michel. "Papa doesn't care. He didn't tell us we had to work today."

"Michel, we can't. I'd like to go fishing or sit in the apple orchard with Jean. We'd talk about the sailing ship that just came to Grand Pré. But we can't. Papa must be very worried, since he isn't working. Many things need to be done, so we'll have to do them."

"You *used* to like to sneak off to go fishing. You're no fun anymore," grumbled Michel.

So we fed the animals, cleaned the barn, and picked carrots and turnips for Maman to cook. We pulled weeds in the vegetable garden. Then we went to help Mme Hébert.

"Why do we have to do Mme Hébert's work? We have enough to do," complained Michel.

"She can't take care of her farm alone, and her children are too small to help," I said. "Acadians take care of their people. We'll help her until Lieutenant-Governor Lawrence lets her husband out of prison." In the evening we milked her cows and ours. All of these things had to be done. I hoped our help would make Papa feel a little bit better.

That evening we sat at the table looking at our food, eating very little. Papa, who usually talked and laughed, spoke only once. "Eat your supper and help Maman clean up," he said. "We're going to Grand-père's house."

Even the little ones, two-year-old Anne, four-year-old Jacques, and six-year-old Brigette were quiet. They looked from one person to the other, not understanding what was happening but knowing that something was wrong.

Oncle Jules, *Tante* (Aunt) Anne, Oncle Auguste, Tante Marie, and all of their children were at Grand-père's house. Whenever we got together, we laughed, talked, played music, and even danced. But that evening we sat without making a sound. That was the first time I could remember when Grand'maman's kitchen didn't smell sweet and spicy with the aroma of a freshly baked cake. She just sat in her rocking chair without saying a word. Grand-père didn't pour spruce beer for the adults. Instead, he said a prayer, and we all joined in.

Oncle Jules said, "We're leaving tonight. We can't live like this any longer. We don't know what Lieutenant-Governor Lawrence is going to do next. Five English ships arrived in the harbor this afternoon. One of the soldiers told me the ships contain food and supplies for the military commander John Winslow. But I know that isn't true, because they're riding high in the water. The ships are empty!"

"Why would Lieutenant-Colonel Winslow need five empty ships?" asked Grand-père.

"I don't know, but I don't trust him," said Oncle Jules.

"Where will you go?" asked Papa.

"We'll sneak into the woods after dark and try to reach *Ile* (Isle) St. Jean. Many of our relatives and neighbors are already there. You must come with us. If we stay here, we'll all be put into prison."

"We're leaving too," said Oncle Auguste. "We have to go to protect the children."

Grand-père shook his head. "Grand'maman and I are too old to walk through the woods at night, hiding from the English soldiers. We'll stay here."

Grand'maman spoke for the first time. "How will you live until you get to Ile St. Jean?"

21

"Our friends the Micmacs will help us," said Oncle Jules. "They'll show us the best route, help us find food, and help us hide. They'll be happy if we escape from the English because they know the English want their land, too."

"We'll stay here until our new baby is born," said Papa. "Marguerite can't travel now, walking through the woods, hiding from the soldiers. We'll join you in a few months."

I wanted to ask questions. I wanted to cry. Why did we have to leave the only home and the only life I had ever known? But I knew better than to ask questions when grown-ups were talking— especially when they were so serious.

I looked at Jean. He always had a smile on his face and a twinkle in his eye. But that night, his shoulders drooped as he stared at the floor. I wasn't sure, but I thought there were tears on his cheeks.

Everyone got up to leave, hugging and crying. Jean and I walked outside together.

"Pierre," said Jean, "let's leave right now. We can go to sea and forget about the English. Lieutenant-Governor Lawrence won't be able to tell us what we can and can't do. I don't want to go to Ile St. Jean."

"I can't, Jean. Maman and Papa will need help traveling with my brothers and sisters, especially with a new baby. Grand-père and Grand'maman might need help, too. I want to sail and get away from our troubles, but I can't go now. I'll meet you after our family is settled. If you're not in Ile St. Jean, I'll search until I find you. I promise, someday we *will* sail together."

"All right, don't forget your promise," said Jean. "I probably will go to the ship tonight, but I wanted to sail with you. I don't want to go to sea without you."

I watched him walk away slowly, his head and shoulders drooping. I had never felt so empty. I wondered if I would ever see him again. I wondered if our lives would ever be the same, or if we would always be running away from someone or something.

5

The Story of the First Acadians

I was lonesome for weeks after Jean and his family left. I woke up every morning, hurrying to get dressed, thinking about something I wanted to tell him. Then I always felt a sinking feeling in my stomach, knowing I might never see him again.

I had other friends, but none like Jean. I thought about him all day, and the things we used to do together. At times, when Papa and I were harvesting our wheat, I'd look toward Jean's farm to see if he was working too. Then I'd remember he was gone. I always said a prayer that he was safe and happy.

One night, Papa asked me to take my brothers and sisters to Grand-père's house. "Ask Grand'maman to come here," he said. "Tell her the baby is coming. Then ask Mme Trahan to come help, too."

We did as we were told and left quickly. Soon the four younger children and I were settled at the table with slices of Grand'maman's cake and glasses of milk. "Grand-père, please tell us how our people came to this land to live." I knew the story, but I wanted my little brothers and sisters to hear it. And I wanted to hear it again so I could remember it forever.

"I'll tell you the story my grand-père told me. You must tell it to your own children and grandchildren. That's the only way it will be remembered.

"Two hundred fifty years ago, only the Micmacs lived in this land. The white men lived far across the ocean. Then, French fishermen began to cross the ocean to fish here in the spring. There were so many fish that the water seemed to be alive. The men spent the whole summer fishing. After they caught the fish, they …"

"I know," I interrupted. "They dried them in the sun or put them in salt in the hold of the ships. That kept the fish from spoiling." Then I blushed because it was very rude to interrupt an adult, especially one as old as Grand-père. "I'm sorry."

Grand-père smiled at me. "I'm glad you remember the story."

"The fishermen went out in small boats to catch the fish," added Michel. "They built platforms near the water to clean and dry them."

"That's right. Then they sailed back to France in the fall with their overloaded ships," continued Grand-père. "They sold the fish to French people who loved the good codfish from our waters. After Cartier claimed this land for France in 1534, the king asked French people to come here to live so no other country could claim the land. England had already claimed land farther south, and Spain wanted some, too. The first men from France settled here in 1605. They lived inside a fort."

"Why did the kings in Europe want land so far away?" asked Michel.

"They hoped to find gold or other treasures," said Grand-père. "The French fishermen knew they could sell dried fish in France. They also brought many furs there. The men liked to wear coats and hats made of beaver skins."

"How did the fishermen get the furs?" asked Michel.

"The Micmacs trapped fur-bearing animals and traded with the fishermen. The fishermen gave the Indians iron cooking pots, knives, hatchets, iron arrow points, kettles, blankets, cloaks, and other things from France."

Anne and Jacques left the table to play with the wooden animals Grand-père had carved for them. He asked me to get his pipe and tobacco from the fireplace mantle. We waited without talking as he filled his pipe and lit it. The sweet fragrance filled the kitchen as Grand-père continued his story.

"My grand'maman and grand-père came to Acadie from France in 1671. The king promised to give land to people who settled here. They lived in Port Royal until 1682 when the people began to receive land grants near Grand Pré.

"My great-great-grand'maman and great-great-grand-père sailed all the way across the ocean," I whispered. "I want to do that someday."

"Yes. The voyage took many weeks. When they arrived, there was so much work to be done that they must have been ready to drop from exhaustion. They had to cut down trees to build houses. Everyone worked together until each family had a place to live. They planted vegetables, built dikes, planted wheat, and raised cows, pigs, sheep, and chickens. The Acadians learned the Micmac way of fishing, using weirs, the way we do today.

"My grand'maman and grand-père had a son a year later, who was my papa. When he got married, he built his house near his papa's, as your papa built your house near mine a few years ago."

"And, God willing, as you will when you are older," said Grand'maman, coming into the house. "Your maman is fine, and you have a beautiful baby sister. Her name is Elizabeth."

A few weeks later, an Indian brought a message to Papa from Oncle Jules and Oncle Auguste. Their trip through the woods was long and hard, but with the Micmacs' help, they made it. They reached Ile St. Jean, and Jean was with them. I wondered why he had decided not to sail. I hoped he was happy.

6

Terrible News

Thursday, September 4, 1755, was a beautiful, cool, sunny day. Papa, Grand-père, Michel, and I were cutting wheat when a messenger came to our farm. He read an order from the military commander, Lieutenant-Colonel John Winslow. "All men, and boys ten years of age and older, are ordered to attend a meeting at Saint-Charles-des-Mines Church in Grand Pré tomorrow afternoon at three o'clock."

I smiled, feeling very grown up. "That means I have to go, too."

Grand-père leaned on his scythe, watching the messenger leave. "I wonder what that's all about."

"Maybe they're going to give our guns back," I said.

Papa shook his head. "I don't think it can be anything good. I don't trust Lieutenant-Governor Lawrence or his officers."

At noon the next day, Papa, Grand-père, and I went to M. Leblanc's house. Many of our neighbors were already there. My friend Isadore stood near the door with his father and two older brothers. They nodded to us but didn't say anything. My friend Julien stood near the fireplace with his father.

7

A Difficult Decision

When the soldiers brought our supper, M. Landry and M. Leblanc sent a message to Lieutenant-Colonel Winslow, asking to meet with him.

"We're worried about our women and children," said M. Landry to Lieutenant-Colonel Winslow. "Please let us go home."

"I'll let twenty men go home tonight," said Winslow. "They'll tell all the women in the village they must supply food and clothes for the prisoners until the ships take you away. The women will also provide food for the soldiers. If all twenty men aren't back by tomorrow morning, their families and all the prisoners will be severely punished."

Papa was chosen to go home overnight, but he asked the soldiers to send me instead. When I left the church, I took a deep breath. I was free! The sky was a brilliant blue, and the air was fresh and clean.

Maman and Grand'maman hugged me so tightly that I could hardly breathe. But I didn't want them to let me go. After I told them the news, I went to tell our neighbors. Many tears were shed, but all of the women said they would do whatever they could for their men.

That night, after Michel fell asleep in our bed in the loft, I made up my mind. I didn't want to be a prisoner. A few hours that afternoon had been enough. I wouldn't let the English soldiers send me away from home. I'd find the Micmacs, and they'd help me get to Ile St. Jean. I'd live with Jean, Oncle Jules, and Tante Anne until Papa and Maman got there. I *would* be free. I *had* to be free.

I rolled up my underwear, socks, extra pair of work clothes, and my church pants. I wrapped everything in my church shirt, and put a few pieces of bread in a clean handkerchief. I didn't need anything else. I crept downstairs, looked around the house for the last time, and went outside. I closed the door without making a sound. I stood in the shadows of the house for a long time, looking and listening, to be sure no one was around.

Everything was quiet. No one was there. I was safe, so far. I had to be more careful than I had ever been. I had to stay away from the English soldiers. I walked through the orchard, staying close to the trunks of the trees, stopping and listening every few minutes. There wasn't a sound.

I looked at our house and barn in the moonlight. Papa, Maman, Grand-père, and Grand'maman never stopped working. Everything— the house, barn, orchards, wheat fields, vegetable garden—was neat and clean.

I slipped into the forest. Suddenly, I stopped. I heard a noise. A rustling sound in the leaves! I stood still in the darkness, breathing so loudly I thought I would wake all the forest animals. Slowly, slowly, I made myself calm down. I listened. Then a little gray squirrel scurried up a tree.

I couldn't believe a little squirrel had frightened me so much. I looked back at my house one more time. I'd made it this far. I was in the forest. I could make it to Ile St. Jean.

I walked on, carefully, the way Little Wolf, my Micmac friend, had taught me. I didn't let a leaf or a branch crack under my feet. I hoped I would find the Micmacs. I needed a friend, especially one who knew the forest well. Maybe I'd find Little Wolf, and he'd come with me.

I was thankful Papa took me outside at night a few years earlier and showed me how to tell directions by looking at the stars. Oncle Jules told Papa his family would travel northeast until they got to the end of Minas Basin, and then they would go north. I knew I'd have to walk through the forest for several days. Then I'd have to find someone with a boat to take me to Ile St. Jean, since it is an island.

I walked on, feeling confident that I could do this. There wasn't a sound in the forest. Suddenly, a hand grabbed my shoulder and another hand covered my mouth. Whoever it was, was behind me, and I couldn't turn around. I couldn't scream because of the hand over my mouth. My heart thudded so hard I thought it would jump out of my chest. I couldn't move; I couldn't even breathe. Would I just collapse and die right there, never knowing who had caught me?

The person behind me pushed me forward without saying a word. He didn't make a sound, walking noiselessly behind me. I wouldn't have known he was there except for the hand pushing me along. He walked like a Micmac, but he must be an English soldier. What was he going to do to me? What was he going to do to my family?

A fire glowed through the trees in a clearing. Teepees! Micmacs! I let out a sigh of relief. I was safe. The man turned me around, and I gazed into the face of Great Wolf, Little Wolf's papa. I was never happier to see anyone in my life—he was a friend. He let go of me as soon as he recognized me.

"Pierre," he said. "Wait here."

He went to a teepee and soon returned followed by a sleepy Little Wolf. My friend was so surprised to see me, he was soon wide-awake. He gave me a big smile. The three of us spoke in a mixture of their native language, gestures, and some French words.

"What are you doing in the forest, alone at night?" Great Wolf asked.

"I'm going to Ile St. Jean. The English soldiers imprisoned all the men and boys in Grand Pré. They're going to send us away, but they won't tell us where."

"We'll help you," said Little Wolf and Great Wolf.

"Sleep on these leaves near the fire," said Great Wolf. "You'll be warm and comfortable. I must guard the tribe for the night, but in the morning, we'll walk with you until we reach other friendly tribes, who will walk farther with you. We know where our enemies, the English soldiers, are. We'll protect you."

I lay down near the fire and tried to sleep, thankful I was with my friends. I wouldn't have to go back to prison. I would reach Ile St. Jean with the Micmacs' help. I'd find Jean, and we'd be sailors. Life was good.

When I closed my eyes, many thoughts went through my head.

Maman and Grand'maman hugging me like they'd never let me go.

Maman, holding the little ones when the English soldiers broke into our house.

Grand'maman, quiet and gentle, smiling at me.

Papa, working from morning to night for his family.

Grand-père, whittling and telling stories to his grandchildren.

The four little ones who need to be protected and cared for.

Michel, working with me because I said the work had to be done. Didn't I tell Michel that helping family and neighbors was more important than having fun? Didn't I tell him Acadians care for their people?

I thought about what the English soldiers had said. Papa, Grand-père, Maman, Grand'maman, the children, and the prisoners would be severely punished if I didn't return to the church in the morning. My stomach turned flip-flops. My throat was dry.

What was I doing? What was I thinking?

Could I give up my freedom? Didn't I deserve to be free?

I got up, picked up my clothes, told Great Wolf where I was going, and quietly walked back into the forest. My Micmac friend went a short way with me and said, "Good luck. If you ever need anything and can send a message to us, we'll help you."

I hurried through the night, moving quietly. I couldn't get caught. Was I doing the right thing? Would I be sorry? It would be many years before I was sure.

8

Waiting

Papa and Grand-père stood near the doors of the church when the soldiers let me in the next morning. I wondered if they were watching for me.

Papa hugged me. "Pierre, I thought you might not come back."

Grand-père put his arm around my shoulders. "I almost hoped you wouldn't come back. I wanted you to be free even if we were punished."

"I walked into the forest last night," I said. "I wanted to run away. Little Wolf and Great Wolf said they would help me. But when I thought about what the soldiers said, that my family and the other prisoners would be severely punished, I had to come back. I couldn't make things worse for you than they already are."

The church was hot and stuffy. Since the windows and doors were shut, there was no fresh air, and we were too crowded to move. The familiar smell of candles and floor wax had changed to the odor of sweaty bodies.

When the women brought our breakfast, the soldiers took some for themselves, and gave the rest to us. The women must have started

Grand'maman, and the children go with us? What about our house, our farm, our animals? Would I ever see Jean and his family again? Should I have gone with him on the sailing ship when we first talked about it? Should I have escaped through the forest when I had the chance? What would the next day and the next weeks bring? None of the prisoners knew what was going to happen to us. The soldiers could not, or would not, tell us anything. I had many questions but no answers.

9

Boarding the Ships

Lieutenant-Colonel Winslow had promised that families wouldn't be separated. But a few days after we were imprisoned, the older boys and unmarried men were ordered to board the five ships anchored near Grand Pré. That would be their prison until the rest of the ships arrived to take us all away.

"Please don't take my boy away," cried M. Trahan. "Let him stay here with me."

"Move," shouted the soldiers to the boy.

Henri Trahan hugged his father, and then joined the older boys as tears rolled down his cheeks.

"Will they make me leave, Papa?" I asked, trying to hide from the soldiers. I shivered until my teeth chattered. Prison was bad enough, but at least I was with Papa and Grand-père. I didn't want to think about going anywhere without them. I was *afraid* to go anywhere without them.

"We can only pray we won't be separated, Pierre," said Papa, putting his arms around me, calming my fears. "We have to do what the soldiers tell us to do. They have guns, and we have no way to defend ourselves."

I was lucky. Lieutenant-Colonel Winslow allowed the younger boys to stay with their fathers. But many families were separated. Some boys refused to leave, but the soldiers, with their guns and bayonets, forced them to obey.

Isadore and his father looked dazed after his two older brothers were taken away. I wanted to talk to them, but nothing I could say would make them feel better. I tried to talk to my friend Julien but couldn't find anything to say. The only time I was at peace was when I was with Papa and Grand-père. We didn't have to talk; I just wanted to be close to them.

About two hundred of us were still imprisoned in church. We were more comfortable with extra room to sit and lie down, but I missed the older boys. I hated seeing the sad faces of the fathers whose sons were gone. They often spoke about their fear that they might never see their boys again. Listening to them always made my heart pound.

I had many questions for Papa and Grand-père.

"Where do you think we will be sent?" I often asked.

"I don't know, son. The soldiers won't tell us anything," said Papa.

"Why did Lieutenant-Colonel Winslow say we could take our money with us? We don't have any money."

"Winslow doesn't know us well enough to know that few Acadians have any money."

"But, Papa, why would we need money?"

"Living the way we do, we don't need it. We raise animals, grow crops, and catch fish so we have all the food we need. We get wool from our sheep and grow flax for the women to spin the thread they use to make cloth on looms; then they make all of our clothes. Friends and neighbors help each other build houses and barns. We even make our own shoes. We trade with the Micmacs, the French, and the English for everything else we need. We are lucky. We don't need money."

On Saturday, October 4, an English soldier who spoke a little French brought our breakfast. "Lieutenant-Colonel Winslow sent soldiers to each house in the village to tell the women to get their food and clothes ready," he said. "The other ships will arrive very soon, and then boarding will begin."

At last we would get out of prison. I wanted to smile, to laugh, but I didn't because everyone looked so serious. We didn't know where we were going to live, but our family would be together again, and we would be free. If we were sent to Ile St. Jean, Louisbourg, or France, we would be happy because we would be with people who shared our language, our religion, and our desire for peace. Maybe we would find Jean and his family and live near them. Nothing would make me happier.

There was a bad storm the following Tuesday. The next day, a soldier had a story for M. Leblanc. "Last night, in the middle of the storm, twenty-four young Acadian men escaped. They had been imprisoned on two of the ships.

"Winslow kept shouting at the soldiers. 'How did this happen? Eight soldiers guard each ship. The crews were there, too.' He was very angry.

"'Sir,' said one of the soldiers. 'We found some men's clothes bundled up and thrown away. The women must have brought dresses and bonnets to the men when they brought their food. The men must have put the clothes on. They escaped dressed as women.'

"'That's the end,' shouted Winslow. 'Tomorrow, the Acadians will begin to board the ships, no matter what the weather is like. We won't wait any longer for the rest of the ships to arrive.'

"Lieutenant-Colonel Winslow sent twenty soldiers to search for the men who escaped," continued the soldier. "They were told to search every house and barn. The men will be sorry they tried to outwit the English soldiers. They'll never try anything like that again when we finish with them."

"What will happen if they aren't found?" asked M. Leblanc.

"Their families will be punished. We'll burn their houses and barns. We'll burn their neighbor's houses and barns. We'll find them."

When M. Leblanc told the story to us, I pictured the young men in dresses and bonnets. I laughed out loud. That was the funniest thing I had heard in a long time. Some of the boys had smiles on their faces, but no one else was laughing.

The next morning, the weather was clear and cold. Two soldiers, who always gave us our orders because they spoke some French, came into the church shouting, "Line up. It's time to board the ships."

"What about our families?" asked Papa.

"Soldiers are going from house to house to tell the women to bring whatever they can carry and go to the landing," replied one of them.

The mile-and-a-half walk from the church to the landing seemed to go on forever. I couldn't wait to see Maman, Grand'maman, Michel, and the little ones. We had been in prison for a month. I wanted to run—to shout for joy. But I couldn't because the soldiers were watching.

The leaves on the trees were red, gold, and yellow. I breathed deeply of the fresh, clean air. A long walk was something familiar. For a few minutes, I could almost imagine everything was back to normal. The apple trees in the orchards were loaded with ripe fruit— yellow and red. I tried to pick a bright red apple, but a shouting soldier carrying a gun pushed me back in line. Then I realized everything was far from normal.

The women walked slowly toward the landing, carrying their babies. People who were too old to walk rode in carts pushed by their children or grandchildren. Some of the carts held furniture. Everyone carried bundles of clothing, food, and household goods, such as pots and dishes. Younger children followed their parents, also carrying bundles. Many of the women were crying.

Suddenly my mouth was dry and my stomach ached, but not from hunger. This wasn't a dream or a game. We were leaving our homes, and we didn't know if we would ever come back.

Five ships were anchored in the Gaspereau River, which flowed into Minas Basin. The other ships Lieutenant-Colonel Winslow had been awaiting were still not in sight. Many small boats were tied up along the shore, with soldiers standing nearby. They began to push women and children into the boats, which carried them to the sailing ships.

Since there were several thousand Acadians in Grand Pré, it took almost six days to load the five ships. Those were days of much confusion. At first the soldiers tried to keep families together, but since women and children were in one group, and men and boys were in another group, it was difficult. And some men and boys were already imprisoned on the ships. Sometimes people were pulled off one ship and put on another in an effort to keep them together, at least at first.

At night, we slept on the bare ground waiting our turn to get on one of the ships. Broken furniture, dishes, and pots covered the shore. The soldiers allowed the women to bring only small bundles of food and clothes onto the ships. There wasn't room for anything else. Some of the soldiers pulled furniture out of the carts and smashed it on the ground.

Mme Hébert carried a small wooden box; a soldier grabbed it and threw it down. "No," she sobbed as it broke into pieces. "That was a wedding present from my husband. He made it for me to keep my handkerchiefs in. He's in prison in Halifax. I'll never see him again, and now I have nothing to remember him by."

Mme Boudrot was on our ship. She cried and screamed when her husband and son were put on another ship.

"Keep quiet, old woman. We can't keep moving everyone from one ship to another. You'll see them when you get off the ship," said one soldier in French.

"I only hope that is true," murmured Papa.

By the grace of God, Papa, Grand-père, and I were put on the same ship as Maman, Grand'maman, and my brothers and sisters. We hugged and said a prayer to thank God we were together. Then we prayed for the families that were separated.

I smiled at everyone on our ship because I was happy we were all together. Knowing how much I missed Jean, I couldn't imagine being separated from my family, alone on a ship, not knowing where we were going. I stopped smiling when I heard cries from one of the other ships. "My children!" screamed a lady. "Please let me find my children."

A soldier pushed her, shouting, "We don't have time to look for children. You'll have to find them later."

Her cries and screams continued. Tears ran down my cheeks as I thought about how lucky our family was to be together.

A few children on our ship had been separated from their parents. They cried bitter tears, but the soldiers didn't try to help them. The Acadians did whatever we could to comfort them. Some families took one or two of the children to watch over and care for.

Once we were on the ships, we waited in our cramped hold for nearly a week for other ships from nearby towns, also filled with Acadians.

When we were imprisoned in the church, waiting to board the ships, I thought everything would be better once we were on our way to our new home. Finally on the ship, I smiled, thinking that my dream of sailing would be realized. Maybe it was a good thing I couldn't foresee what our lives would be like for the next few years. If I had known, I wouldn't have been able to smile.

Part Three
The Ships
October-November 1755

CANADA

St. Lawrence River

Ile St. Jean

Nova Scotia

(Acadie)

Quebec

Colonies

Maryland

Annapolis

ATLANTIC OCEAN

ENGLISH TERRITORY

American

SPANISH TERRITORY

Mississippi River

From ACADIE

to MARYLAND

1755

to LOUISIANA

1766

LOUISIANA

New Orleans

GULF OF MEXICO

Saint Domingue

10

Nothing Left

On Tuesday, October 21, the five ships from Grand Pré began to move slowly away from land as wind filled their sails. The deck was crowded with many of our friends and relatives. I was sailing, at last. The wind ruffled my hair. The ship rocked gently. I took deep breaths of the salty air. I smiled, and then my eyes filled with tears. This had been my dream for so long, but this was not the way I had planned it. I wanted to sail with Jean, and then come back to my family and my home in Grand Pré, to my life the way it had always been. For the first time I realized that would never happen.

The soldiers pushed us toward the hold of the ship as we sailed into Minas Basin.

"Look!" shouted M. Martin, pointing toward the shore. "Fire!"

"No," groaned M. Thibodeau. "Our houses are on fire!"

"Now we'll have nothing to come back to," whispered Papa.

As we watched, people on the other ships shouted and cried. My heart sank. Something must be terribly wrong.

"What is happening, Papa?" I asked.

"The soldiers are burning our houses and barns. They don't want us to come back to Acadie—*ever*," he said, with his voice breaking.

"What about our animals? Where are our dogs? What will happen to our cows, sheep, and pigs? And what about our wheat and our fruit trees?"

A soldier standing near us snarled, "We took your animals and the harvested wheat. We took whatever we could use from your houses. That will help to repay the English government for the cost and trouble of moving you."

"We built our houses with the help of our neighbors," murmured Grand-père. "My grand-père and the men in the village built our church long before I was born. It must be gone too."

I watched as the flames grew and spread. The wheat in the fields began to burn with thick, black smoke. Soon everything would be gone except the smoke.

Tears ran down the cheeks of men as well as women and children. Shoulders shook and people sobbed. I began to realize how terrible this was. I had never felt so empty in my whole life. This was worse than being separated from Jean, worse than losing my gun, worse than being locked up in church, and even worse than leaving Acadie. Our houses, our furniture, our barns, our crops, and our animals were gone. Everything was gone. How could we ever come back? My throat hurt so much, I could hardly swallow. Tears ran down my face, and I couldn't stop them. I didn't try to stop them.

We watched in silence until the soldiers sent us down into the hold of the ship.

"What is going to happen to us?" I cried. "Will our lives ever be the same? Will we ever be happy again?"

"Pierre, as bad as things are right now, at least we are together," said Grand-père as he wiped his tears. "Never forget what we have always told you. As long as we can stay together, we will survive." He put his arm around my shoulders, and, together, we climbed down the ladder into the dark hold of the ship.

11

Another Prison

Whenever I closed my eyes, I saw our houses and barns burning until nothing was left. The smoky smell seemed to cling to my skin and clothes. I thought of our house, with its wooden walls and its roof made of a thick layer of mud with marsh grass growing on it. The house had been clean and bright, with one big room at the bottom and a loft overhead, where Michel and I slept. Jacques would have slept up there with us when he was older. A big stone fireplace had kept the house warm and was the place where Maman cooked. Her bread, cakes, and soup had always smelled and tasted delicious. It had been a happy house, where we talked, laughed, and had fun.

I couldn't sleep and couldn't stop thinking about everything we had lost. When I was in prison in our church, I had looked forward to this journey. After all, I did want to be a ship's boy. This was my chance to sail. But I had never thought a ship could be another prison. We couldn't even talk to most of our friends who were sailing with us. The hold was divided into compartments, and we saw only the people in our small group. And the soldiers allowed only a few people at a time to leave the dark hold to walk on deck for several minutes every day.

"Papa, why can't we visit with our other friends on the ship?" I asked.

M. Martin heard my question. "The guards are afraid we might try to take over the ship if a number of us are on deck together."

But after a short time on the ship with almost no exercise and little to eat, everyone was so weak and tired that we couldn't have fought if we had wanted to.

A few days after we sailed, I had just climbed out of the hold with Papa when the fluttering of white sails caught my eye. Many ships had joined the five that had left Grand Pré.

"Where are they going, Papa?" I asked.

"I don't know. Maybe the captain will tell M. Martin, since he speaks English."

Later, M. Martin came back from his walk on the deck. "The ships are from Chignecto, another part of Acadie. The Acadians there were also forced to leave their homes."

After we sailed into the Bay of Fundy, there was a terrible storm. The soldiers wouldn't let us leave the hold, so we sat in the dark, tossed from side to side as the ship moved through the water. Everyone slid to one side of the ship as it was thrown around by the waves. Moments later, we all slid to the other side, with people piling on top of one another. The roar of the storm was so loud I couldn't hear Michel when he spoke right next to my ear. Because we were all so frightened, people cried out loudly at times. Frigid water from the terrible waves seeped through the cracks in the deck until we were all wet and shivering.

"What's going to happen to us?" I shouted. But no one answered. Probably no one heard me, and no one knew the answer.

Never had I been so miserable or so afraid. With the ship tossing around wildly, even if I could have stood up, my legs wouldn't have held me. I was sure the ship would break apart any minute, and we would all drown. Or maybe we would sink to the bottom of the bay, waiting for the ship to fill with water, and then we would drown. I couldn't talk to Papa or Grand-père about my fears because of the roar of the storm.

Even though a number of Acadians were crowded into that dark hold, I felt very much alone. That is, until three-year-old Antoine climbed onto my lap. He and his five-year-old sister, Emilie, were separated from their parents in Grand Pré when we boarded the ship. We heard their parents pleading with the soldiers, but it didn't do any good. They were shoved onto another ship, and we could only hope and pray we would find them at the end of our voyage.

Antoine clung to me. I couldn't scream because of fear or anger, or both, even though I wanted to very much. I had to be strong for him. When Emilie climbed on Grand'maman's lap, the little girl's cries changed to quiet tears.

Many people were seasick, but there was no help for them. At times my stomach felt like it was turning upside down, but with so little food in it, I didn't get sick. After several miserable days, the water and the wind finally quieted.

The storm was over, and I left the hold, breathing deeply for the first time in many days, trying to forget the smell of burning wood and crops. I was surprised I was still alive. I was glad I was still alive. I even felt a tiny stirring of hope that someday I might be happy again.

I held Antoine's tiny hand and pointed to the birds flying overhead. The sky was a brilliant blue. The sun sparkled on the waves. A fish jumped out of the water, then hurriedly dove back in. That brought a quick smile to Antoine's chubby, tear-streaked face.

I looked for the other ships carrying Acadians, but not one was in sight. I wondered if they had sunk in the storm. I thought about my friends and our neighbors who had boarded those ships, but I couldn't cry. I couldn't take any more sadness. I just had to get through each day, one day at a time.

When Papa came back after his walk on deck, he said, "The captain of our ship told M. Martin he has never taken a ship through such a terrible storm before. He was afraid we'd sink. We're lucky he's a good sailor. We're also lucky M. Martin speaks English, so he and the captain can talk. But the captain couldn't, or wouldn't, tell him where we're going."

The storm was over, but the roar of the water crashing against the wooden hull was still deafening. Michel could stand up in the hold, but adults had to stoop. When I tried to stand up straight, I bumped my head on the ceiling and let out a little yell.

We had no light, no windows. During the day we sat in the dark, except for the light that crept through the cracks in the ship's deck, which was our ceiling. Sometimes the soldiers left the door to the hold open. Then we were thankful we could see a little in the dimness.

"Why can't we light a candle, Papa?" I asked one day. "We'd be happier if we could see each other."

"With the ship rocking in the waves, a candle could start a fire. We'd all die down here in the bottom of this ship," answered Papa.

We were always cold. The air was musty and damp. At times it was hard to breathe. We were active people, and it was difficult to sit or lie down day and night without moving around. We didn't have enough food or water; we had no privacy and no sanitation. The smell of sickness, unwashed bodies, and wet clothes was terrible. The Acadian women had always taken pride in keeping themselves, their children, and their houses clean. Now there was no way to keep clean. We had so little water we had to save it for drinking. We couldn't waste it washing hands, faces, or clothes. Maman and Grand'maman must have been miserable, but they didn't complain.

Days on the ship were long, but nights were even longer. We were so crowded, there wasn't enough room for everyone to lie down at the same time. We had to take turns sleeping. Half of the people would lie down on the floor of the ship while the others sat up. I hated sitting in the dark when many people were asleep. I couldn't see the stars. The sailors were always quiet at night; most of them were probably asleep. So there was nothing for me to do except think about my life—as it had been in Acadie, and as it was aboard the ship. I hoped God was listening when I prayed.

At first, whenever I went up on deck, I had trouble walking. I held on to the rail because I was afraid I'd fall as the ship rocked from side to side in the waves. I smiled my first real smile since I boarded the ship when I finally learned to walk like a sailor, without holding on.

Once when I left the hold for my daily walk, I stood near the rail. The wind blew my hair and cooled my face. Water and sky stretched in all directions with nothing else in sight. The water was calm and blue. The ship's white sails stood straight and tall. A few puffy clouds decorated the bright blue sky. I licked my lips and tasted salt from the spray of the sea.

A sailor gestured to me, asking for help with one of the sails. I felt free. This was what Jean and I had planned to do with our lives. I felt happy for the first time in days.

But soon a guard called to me. "Go back down in the hold, boy. You've been on deck too long."

Slowly, I went down the ladder into the damp, smelly hold, which was filled with sadness.

12

Hunger

"**W**e had a good life in Acadie, didn't we?" said Mme Thibodeau one day. "We should talk about it more often so we'll always remember. I don't want my children to ever forget that they're Acadians."

"Yes, it was good," replied Mme Martin. "We worked hard caring for the children, cooking, cleaning, sewing, spinning thread, weaving cloth, and helping the men in the fields at harvest time. We were always busy, but we were happy. I miss it so much."

"Do you remember how we used to sing when we cut the wheat?" asked Mme Boudrot, speaking for the first time since she was separated from her husband and son. "We also sang when we worked in our gardens and orchards, picking fruit or pruning trees. Our children piled fruit into baskets, then ran and played under the trees."

"I miss going to church when we met on Sundays and Holy Days to pray," said Grand'maman. "I looked forward to attending Mass whenever a priest visited our area. We had wonderful celebrations for our children's weddings and their babies' baptisms."

"I liked Saturdays best of all," said Mme Hébert. "I'd go to the village in the morning to trade our crops and visit with friends. Then on Saturday nights, it was such fun to get together to sing and dance at someone's house."

"I liked to eat the food everyone brought," said Michel.

Maman smiled at him. "I enjoyed watching everyone dance, even the youngest children."

"I feel better now," said Mme Boudrot. "We need to talk about good things more often."

I was glad Mme Boudrot felt better because she often cried for her husband and son. But I had a sinking feeling in the pit of my stomach again. Talking about our lives made me think of the bright red flames and the thick black smoke.

"Papa, I don't know why I wanted to leave home to be a ship's boy," I said. "I'll never be as happy as I was in Acadie."

"That's the way people are, son. We always think something else will be better than what we already have."

* * *

Maman and Grand'maman had brought apples and pears for us to eat, as many as they could carry. In the middle of our second week on the ship, enough fruit was left for each child to have just one more piece. Even though the grown-ups couldn't have any, I wanted my whole apple. Just as I took the first bite, the ship lurched, and the fruit rolled between the legs and feet of the people sitting near us. My friend Julien picked up my juicy, red apple and took a big bite.

"What are you doing?" I yelled. "That's my apple, my last one. Who knows when I'll ever have another one?" I made a fist and was ready to punch him.

He spoke in a whisper. "I just took one bite. I was going to give the rest to my little brother, Charles. He's so sick. Maybe this will help him get stronger so he won't die. He refuses to eat the dry bread and salt pork the soldiers give us."

Five-year-old Charles lay across his mother's lap. He was as pale as her white apron. His eyes were closed, and he was breathing fast.

"Give him the apple," I said. "I wish I had something else for him to eat. Maybe Maman or Grand'maman has some medicine to make him feel better."

Maman had brought leaves from plants the Micmacs taught her to use when someone was sick. She mixed some with a little water from the wooden bucket holding our drinking water and gave it to Charles. I hoped he'd feel better. I sat quietly and thought about the way I had acted. I was ashamed of myself. I stared at the floor. I couldn't look anyone in the eye. Maman and Papa always taught us to share whatever we had. What was happening to me? I was hungry, but so was everyone else.

After we finished Maman and Grand'maman's fruit and dried fish, we had to eat the ship's food. The soldiers gave each of us a small piece of hard, dry bread in the morning, and another with a small piece of salt pork in the evening. There was never enough. We were always hungry. I dreaded the sound of babies crying because their stomachs ached from hunger. But it was even worse when they stopped crying. They just looked at the adults with pleading eyes, as if silently begging for something to eat.

13

Sickness

M ore people got sick, and some died.
"Papa, why are so many people sick?" I asked. "We were never sick before."

"Pierre, we were healthy because we worked hard in the fresh air and sunshine," said Papa. "We had good food to eat—as much as we wanted. We always had fish, meat, lots of fresh vegetables from the garden, and fruit from the orchard."

"Even in the winter, our attic was filled with dried fish and meat, dried peas, beans, and apples," said Maman. "We also had food in the cellar—turnips, onions, corn, and more apples."

"We were never hungry," said Papa. "We lived a good life, so we were strong and healthy. Here, we have no fresh air, little food, stale water, and no room to move around. It's not a healthy way to live."

My mouth began to water. "I dream about cabbages and turnips. Maman, you made such delicious soups and stews every day. If we were at home, it would soon be time for us to cut our cabbages."

Michel looked at me. "Remember how we left them on the ground with the stalks up? The snow covered them and protected them all winter. We had cabbage whenever we wanted it. I wish I could go into our yard right now and bring in some vegetables for Maman to cook."

"I'd like nothing better than to cook for you again," Maman said softly.

"We ate a lot of fish, didn't we?" said Mme Thibodeau. "Since the Catholic Church forbids eating meat on Fridays and many other days of the year, our children got tired of eating salted and dried fish when they couldn't catch any."

"They complained," said Mme Martin. "But they didn't know what it was like to be hungry, until now."

Four-year-old Jacques climbed on Maman's lap. "Maman, if someone would give me some fresh fish right now, I'd never complain again. I'm *so* hungry."

I stood up. "I'm going up on deck to catch some fish. I'm sure I'll find a pole and bait. Yesterday one of the sailors was cooking codfish. The smell reminded me of home. It made me so hungry that I wanted to grab a piece of fish and run off to eat it."

"If you catch something, how will you cook it?" asked Michel. "I don't want any raw fish."

"The sailors' stove is on deck. It's a metal box sitting in a box of sand. I know they'll let me catch some fish and cook them if I tell them the children are hungry."

"The soldiers won't let you," said Papa.

"I'm going to try."

The trapdoor was open, so I climbed up the ladder. The first soldier who saw me began to shout. "What are you doing up here? You're supposed to stay down below until you're called."

"I want to catch some fish. Everyone is starving, especially the children. I'll share the fish I catch with you and the sailors, if we can cook them on your stove."

"Don't try to bribe me, boy. Get back where you belong. And no bread for you tomorrow." The soldier pushed me, and I could do nothing except go back to the damp, smelly hold.

"I'm sorry, Jacques. The soldier on guard duty won't let me catch any fish."

"You can have my bread tomorrow," he said. "I don't think I'm going to be hungry."

I gave him a big hug. "Thank you, Jacques, but I don't think I'll be hungry either."

14

Pleasant Memories and Promises

The next day, Grand-père was quiet and looked sadder than usual.

"What's wrong?" asked Grand'maman. "Are you sick?"

"No," said Grand-père. "I'm tired of sitting here. I'm used to working in the fields, taking care of the animals, and doing other chores. I can't even keep my hands busy because I don't have my knife or any wood to whittle."

"Oh, Grand-père," I said, "the animals you made for us are gone. I always played with them when I was Jacques's age."

"I keep thinking about the cradle you made, Grand-père," said Maman. "Your babies all slept in it. You gave it to us before Pierre was born, and all of our babies slept in it. I wanted to keep it for my grandchildren and great-grandchildren, but I couldn't bring it on the ship. And now it's gone." Her voice broke on the last word as she wiped her tears away. That made me sadder than I was before.

Grand-père took Maman's hand. "Marguerite, I'll make another cradle for your grandchildren and great-grandchildren. And Pierre, I'll whittle so many animals, you won't know where to put them.

That's my promise to all of you, as soon as we are settled again. The cradle won't be old but it will be made with love. And the animals will be better than the others because I've had a lot of practice."

"Thank you." Maman kissed Grand-père's cheek, smiling through her tears. Then she kissed Grand'maman and said, "I brought one thing with me that I'll always treasure. It's the beautiful lacy wedding handkerchief you made for me. It's the only thing I have, besides my wonderful family, to remind me of our life in Acadie."

"Oh, Maman, please show me the handkerchief and tell us the story about when you and Papa got married," said six-year-old Brigette.

"It was a beautiful day in October after the wheat was harvested," began Maman. "Acadian weddings were almost always between October and February because the work in the fields was finished. Ours was at Saint-Charles-des-Mines, our little church in the village. I wore the long Sunday skirt I made from wool from our own sheep. It was black with stripes of red yarn my papa got from an English ship. He traded some wheat for the yarn because he knew I loved red so much. Your papa wore his Sunday jacket and breeches.

"After the wedding, we went to Grand'maman and Grand-père's house to eat a delicious cake that Grand'maman made. Then our friends walked with us to the house they had helped Papa build for us. They had also helped him clear the land and plant some wheat. Our wedding gifts were two calves, some pigs, chickens, and seeds for our wheat field and vegetable garden. My maman gave me a mattress stuffed with soft goose feathers and some cuttings from her fruit orchard so I could plant my own trees.

"Those fruit trees grew tall and strong. We all enjoyed eating ripe apples, pears, and cherries from our own trees."

Michel licked his lips. "Don't forget the fruit pies you made."

"And the preserves and jelly," I added.

"I liked to climb those trees," said Michel. "Then I could look down and watch everyone."

I smiled at him. "You dropped apple cores and cherry pits on Jean and me when we sat in the shade to cool off after working in the fields."

"That was the most fun of all."

"You knew we couldn't climb quite as high as you could because you're lighter and smaller."

"So you couldn't catch me," laughed Michel.

"The three of you were always up to something," said Papa, putting his arms around Michel and me.

That night, I fell asleep with a smile on my face. I relaxed for a little while, for the first time since our long walk to church on September 5, the day the men and boys in Grand Pré were imprisoned. So much had happened since that day. It was barely two and a half months, but it seemed like forever.

15

Journey's End

As the days passed, we talked less and less. No one smiled. No one laughed. We still held hands and said our morning and evening prayers together every day, then sang a hymn or two. Many people just sat the rest of the day with their eyes closed, or they stared at nothing at all.

Darkness surrounded us. Sadness pressed down like a heavy weight until I could hardly breathe. Sometimes I couldn't remember ever being happy. "Maman," I said, "I don't think any of us will ever get off this ship. But it doesn't matter anymore."

Maman put her arms around me. "My dear child, you've been so strong. We must keep remembering the good life we had. It will be good again. You'll see."

That night, I dreamed I was back in Acadie. Jean and I raced across the meadow. The sky was a brilliant blue, and the sun was warm on our backs. We ran until we couldn't take another step, and then tumbled down in the shade of a cherry tree. We reached up to the low-hanging branches and ate juicy cherries until our stomachs couldn't hold any more. I closed my eyes, listening to the chattering birds and buzzing bees.

Suddenly, I opened my eyes and looked around. At first, I didn't know where I was. Instead of the brightness of the sun, I saw only darkness. I didn't hear a sound. Then I knew I had been dreaming. I was still on the ship sailing farther and farther away from home. Nobody knew where we were going. But something was different. What was it? Suddenly I realized the ship wasn't moving! Why had we stopped?

Others began to wake up, and everyone had a question.

"Why aren't we moving?"

"Is something wrong?"

"Have we finally reached our destination?"

M. Martin banged on the trapdoor that opened to the deck. A soldier came to the door but didn't give much information.

"What is happening?" asked M. Martin.

"We've reached the place where the captain was paid to bring you. We can finally get rid of you people," replied the soldier.

"Where are we?"

"You'll be told what you need to know." The door slammed shut.

Everyone started talking.

"Where can we be?"

"I hope the people here speak French and are Catholics."

"I hope the land is good for farming."

"I hope all of the other ships from Acadie are here."

"I can't wait to find my husband and son."

"I want Maman and Papa."

"I can't wait to get off this ship."

"I can't wait for some good food."

"Thank God we arrived safely." We held hands and said a prayer of thanks.

I sat in the dark, wondering what was happening. My stomach was turning flip-flops. I was sweating, even though it was cold in the hold of the ship. What was wrong with me? I had gotten used to the movement of the ship, the crowding, the darkness, the lack of food, the terrible-tasting water, the smell of sickness and unwashed people. Even seeing my friends and neighbors getting sick and dying was no longer unusual. As bad as all of that was, it was familiar. I was afraid because, once more, I didn't know what was going to happen.

Was our life finally going to get better? Or could it get worse? Was that possible? The only thing I could do was hold on to Antoine. I tried to comfort him as I gained strength from the tight grip of his little hand.

Part Four
Maryland
Winter 1755–66

16

Land at Last

Days crept by. Everything was the same, except our ship was sitting in the harbor instead of sailing. We didn't know where we were. We sat in the dark hold and waited and wondered. What was going to happen to us?

When I took my daily walk on the deck, I had to smile. There were trees in the distance. For over a month I had seen nothing except water and sky and smelled nothing but the salty spray of the water. It was wonderful to see trees. But I wanted spring to come so I could sit in the cool shade, listen to birds chirping among the leaves, and smell the sweet blossoms while waiting for the taste of juicy fruit.

M. Martin stood with me near the rail for a few minutes, then called to a friendly sailor. I couldn't understand what they were saying, but waited for M. Martin to go back into the hold where he told us what he had learned.

"We're anchored in Chesapeake Bay," said M. Martin. "We're going to live in Maryland, one of the American colonies."

"Why can't we get off the ship if this is where we're going to live?" asked Papa.

"The governor of Maryland didn't know several shiploads of people were coming here to live until the first ship arrived a few days ago. Yesterday, the captain brought a letter to him from Lieutenant-Governor Lawrence. We have to stay on the ship until the governor decides what to do with us."

"Do you think the people will welcome us?" asked Maman.

"I don't know," said M. Martin. "These people are English, and they hate the French because the two countries have been at war for years. But the sailor thinks we're probably luckier than Acadians who are going to live in other English colonies. There are some Catholics in Maryland, and they might accept us. Protestants live in the other colonies, and they don't like Catholics."

"I've lost track of time," I said. "How long have we been on this ship?"

"Nearly seven weeks. Today is November 30, 1755," said M. Martin.

"Are any other ships here from Grand Pré?" asked Papa.

M. Martin nodded. "Three ships filled with Acadians arrived before we did. One of them is from Grand Pré. Those people are also waiting for permission from the governor to go ashore."

"What about all the other ships that left Acadie?"

"The only thing the sailor knew is that they were heading to other American colonies. He said Lieutenant-Governor Lawrence wants to separate us so we'll never be strong enough to fight the English."

Finally one evening, instead of bringing our supper, a soldier brought the news we had been waiting for. "Come on. Hurry up. You're going to stay in the town of Annapolis. You have to get off the ship right now. We're getting ready to sail. We can't stay here forever."

Even if the soldier had brought our usual supper of salt pork and dry bread, I couldn't have swallowed it. I was too excited—and scared. Dry bread wouldn't have gone past the big lump in my throat.

It felt strange to walk on land instead of on the swaying ship. I took a deep breath of the cold, fresh air. I looked around, gave thanks, and prayed we would be happy.

I turned to see if people were getting off the other ships and saw all three sailing away. "The other ships. Where are they going?"

A man in the crowd answered, "One of the sailors told me they're going to other towns in Maryland. The people of Annapolis don't want to have to support nearly nine hundred refugees."

My heart dropped as I watched the ships getting smaller and smaller in the distance. If those people had been allowed to stay in Annapolis, there was a chance we would find Emilie and Antoine's parents.

There was a lot of confusion on the dock because our ship had held nearly two hundred people. Everyone was looking for family and friends, hoping they had been in another part of our ship. Some people walked around shouting the names of their lost relatives.

We walked through the noisy crowd, looking for friends. Antoine held my hand so tightly his little fingernails dug into my skin. Maman carried Baby Elizabeth and held Emilie's hand. Papa held on to Anne and Jacques. Michel and Brigette followed closely behind, holding hands.

"Stay close together, children. We don't want to lose any of you," said Maman.

"There's Mme Hébert," I shouted. "But where are Grand'maman and Grand-père? I don't see them following us." My heart sank.

Papa turned around to look. "Oh, no. I thought they were right behind us. We must have gotten separated in the crowd." We looked for them, and called their names over and over, but we couldn't find them. Brigette and Jacques started to cry.

Papa said, "I'll find them, no matter how long it takes." I wanted to tell him I would help, but I couldn't make a sound. If I had tried to talk, I would have cried instead. As long as I could remember, I had visited Grand'maman and Grand-père every day. How could I live without seeing their kind, smiling faces? I depended on Grand-père's good advice and Grand'maman's hugs.

It was already getting dark, and the weather was bitterly cold. It was snowing hard and a strong wind blew. We had left home in the fall, when the weather was cool and pleasant. Now our shoes and clothes weren't heavy enough to keep us warm. We didn't have coats or gloves, and the wind blew right through our clothes. My fingers were soon numb, so I couldn't feel Antoine's cold hand in mine.

Everyone looked sad, dirty, thin, and pale. Clothes were torn and stained. No one looked like the happy, clean, well-fed people I knew.

Soldiers pointed, and pushed us toward a big building. M. Thibodeau stood inside. "The local ministers promised to help every family find a place to live," he said. "We'll be allowed to stay in this building until we find homes. The ministers collected jackets from the townspeople for us. There should be enough for everyone."

We wandered around, looking for Grand'maman and Grand-père. Everyone seemed to be looking for someone. The building was cold, but it was warmer than walking in the snow. I felt warm inside whenever I recognized friends and neighbors. There were some I hadn't seen since we left Grand Pré because we had been cramped into different parts of the ship and took our walks on deck at different times. We hugged and smiled through our tears. Maybe we could be happy again.

We soon had to stop walking around because it was too dark to see. I wondered what was going to happen to us. I prayed that we would find Grand'maman and Grand-père. I prayed that we would find a place to live.

17

A New Friend

The building grew colder, so we huddled together to keep warm as the wind whistled outside. The sailors brought buckets of water, and the dry bread from the ship. "After this," one of them said to M. Martin, "you'll have to find your own food. Our ship sails early tomorrow morning."

I couldn't eat. I couldn't swallow another piece of dry bread.

In the morning a group of people, speaking English, came into the building. That was the language of the men who had driven us from our homes. I gritted my teeth, wondering if they would be as cruel as Lieutenant-Governor Lawrence and his soldiers had been.

A lady went to M. Martin and spoke to him. They looked around, then moved toward the corner of the room where my family stood.

M. Martin said, "This is Mrs. Adams. She has an empty shed where she and her husband lived when they got married, forty years ago. Her husband died last year, after they built their house. She'll let you stay in the shed until you find another place to live. She is sorry for the way we were treated by the English, and she wants to help."

Mrs. Adams spoke to M. Martin in English. "She said the shed is in poor shape," M. Martin told us.

"It's a place to live. It will be better than the ship or this building," said Papa. "Please thank her for us."

M. Martin walked with us to help us get settled. As we followed Mrs. Adams to our new home, I wondered what our life would be like. If it's not better, I thought, I *will* be a ship's boy. I'll sail to Ile St. Jean and find my cousin Jean. We'll sail together as we promised each other months ago.

We trudged a long way in the snow following Mrs. Adams. The houses in town stood in rows, close together. Outside of town, people had a little more land, where they could raise animals or grow crops.

My fingers and toes were freezing. We were all shivering, and the little ones were crying by the time we reached Mrs. Adams's house. The shed in her backyard had one long room. In it were a fireplace, an old table, benches, and a few pots and dishes. It was very cold because of several holes in the roof and the walls.

Mrs. Adams showed Papa the pile of firewood outside. He soon had a fire roaring in the fireplace. We stood close, trying to get warm, trying to get feeling back into our fingers and toes. "Mrs. Adams has a small barn for her cow and some chickens," said Papa. "Maybe she will let us work for milk and eggs."

Before M. Martin left, Mrs. Adams gave us blankets, half a loaf of bread, and a pitcher of milk. "I'm sorry—it's not much, but it's all I have."

"Merci," we all said together.

For the first time in weeks, we ate fresh bread instead of hard, dry bread. And sweet, fresh milk instead of water. What a feast that was! I ate and drank slowly to make mine last a long time.

Finally we were warm and dry. We had a place to live. While we were on the ship, I thought my heart was frozen, and I'd never be happy again. But because of Mrs. Adams, I felt a little flutter of happiness inside. She wanted to help us, sharing the little she had. Maybe other people would be kind to us, too.

"I think Mrs. Adams is an angel," said Antoine. We laughed, but from then on, we called her *Mme Ange* (Mrs. Angel) instead of Mrs. Adams. In the next weeks and months, Mme Ange was so kind to us, we became good friends. Since we wanted to talk to her, my family learned a little English, and she learned a little French. We didn't hate the sound of the English language when it came from her lips.

18

A Place to Live

We were getting settled in the shed that was going to be our home, and I was finally feeling warm when Papa walked to the door. "Come on, Pierre. We'd better try to find some firewood and some food. Mme Ange has just enough firewood for herself, and we can't depend on her to feed us."

"May I come, too?" begged Michel.

"Yes, you may help."

So we went out into the cold again. "I didn't think anyone in my family would ever have to beg for food," said Papa. "I thought if we worked hard we'd always have everything we needed."

I shuffled through the snow, following him. "I *can't* beg, Papa. I wouldn't be able to open my mouth. I'd be too embarrassed."

"Are you hungry, Pierre?"

"Yes, Papa."

"Do you think your maman and your little brothers and sisters are hungry?"

"Yes, Papa."

"Have you noticed how pale and thin they are?"

"Yes, Papa."

"Do you want them to get sick and die because they have nothing to eat?"

"No, Papa."

"Then you'd better beg for food until we can find jobs."

So I begged. Even though I was weak from hunger, I was still embarrassed. I had to keep reminding myself that Maman, Antoine, Emilie, and my brothers and sisters were half-starved. My face turned bright red, and I stumbled over the words, but I went with Papa and Michel from house to house saying, "Please give us something to eat."

One lady gave Michel half a loaf of bread. Another gave me three carrots and a small cabbage. Her neighbor gave me an onion and a few turnips.

But several shouted, "Go away!" They waved their arms, gesturing for us to leave, and slammed the door in our faces. That was worse than having to beg. I wanted to hide. I felt about one foot tall.

Papa found an armload of wood, enough to last a few days. "Let's go back, boys. We need to get warm again. This is enough for today."

As I trudged back through the snow following Papa and Michel, I looked at the carrots I was carrying. No one would know if I ate one. Papa didn't know how many the lady had given me. He wouldn't know one was missing. My stomach hurt because I was so hungry. I hadn't eaten any vegetables for almost two months. My mouth watered. I took a big bite. The carrot was sweet and tender. It was delicious.

I started to take another bite. Then I thought of Maman, who had been eating almost nothing so she could share the little food she had with us. I thought of Antoine and the other children with their sad faces, and how thin and pale they were. I couldn't swallow another bite of that delicious carrot.

Everyone was delighted to see the vegetables. The children held hands and danced around the room, laughing and shouting.

Maman said, "I'll make soup. It won't taste very good without meat to flavor it. But it will be more than we've had for a long time." If she noticed that one of the carrots had a bite missing, she didn't say anything.

The smell of hot, fresh bread and Maman's soup made the shed feel more like home. That was the best meal I'd ever eaten, even without meat, peas, and other vegetables Maman usually put in. We ate until nothing was left, then said our prayers, thankful for food to eat, fire in the fireplace, and Mme Ange's blankets.

Before I went to sleep on the floor near the fireplace, I thought about how much luckier I was than many Acadians. I still remembered the cries and screams of so many who had been separated from their families. I was with Maman, Papa, and my little brothers and sisters. We had a place to live and a new friend, Mme Ange. I was warm inside and out. My stomach was full. But a little empty place inside was a reminder that we didn't know where Grand'maman and Grand-père were.

I woke up during the night feeling something cold and wet on my face. I touched my cheek and the blanket. Then I realized what it was. Snow! The others soon woke up, and we moved our blankets nearer the fireplace. I shivered, then pulled Antoine and Michel closer as we tried to keep warm together.

In the morning, Papa looked at the roof and the walls. There was one big hole in the roof, a few smaller ones, and a pile of snow in the house.

Papa added wood to the glowing embers in the fireplace. "Come on, Pierre. We'd better fix the roof." He borrowed tools from Mme Ange. Soon we were on the freezing, snowy roof in our thin, raggedy clothes, patching holes with some of the wood Papa had found the day before. After that we were much warmer, without the winter wind and snow blowing into the room. We still had enough wood for a small fire in the fireplace.

After the roof was fixed, Papa said, "Marguerite, you'd better try to find some food today. Pierre, Michel, and I must look for work."

So poor Maman had to beg for food while we looked for jobs. It took nearly two weeks, but Papa finally found a man who needed help on his farm. The farmer hired Michel and me to cut wood and run errands. He promised to pay us with food for the family.

"Just think, Papa," I said, smiling. "We won't have to beg for food anymore."

He looked at me. "We need warm clothes and shoes, too. I don't know how I'll get everything we need."

When we arrived home, the mouth-watering smell of hot soup and fresh, hot bread greeted us. I forgot everything—the cold weather, hard work, and the things our family needed. I just enjoyed the taste of Maman's good food again.

19

More Changes

Since we couldn't pay rent for the shed, we helped Mme Ange as much as we could. Michel and I milked her cow, cleaned the barn, and fed the chickens. Papa fixed her roof and filled the cracks in her house so it would be warmer in winter. Maman brought soup or stew to her several times a week. And kind Mme Ange gave us a pitcher of milk every time we milked her cow.

I was grateful we had a place to live, a new friend, and food to eat. But while I cut wood for the farmer, I often thought of everything we had lost. In Acadie we had never been hungry, we had lots of different kinds of food to eat, and we had many friends and relatives. We had a nice place to live and time for fun. That big, hollow place in the pit of my stomach made me want to cry. I wanted my happy life again.

Michel dragged his feet on the way home from work one day. "Why do people hate us so much, Papa? We didn't do anything to them."

Papa put his arm around Michel's shoulders. "Many people have been unkind to us. The English people hate the French because the two countries have been at war for such a long time. Since we speak French, they hate us."

"Then why don't we hate them?"

"We don't hate anyone. That's not our way."

"Does everyone hate us?"

"No, some people seem to respect us because we work hard and live simply, but many others don't want us here. They complain about the Acadians who can't find work. Our people aren't lazy—no one wants to hire them. Unfortunately, some of our people are dying because they don't have enough food or a warm place to live. Not many people have a wonderful friend like Mme Ange who is willing to help them."

I sighed, wondering how long we would survive. I could hardly remember a time when I wasn't exhausted, hungry, and sad. The faces of our Acadian friends had the pinched, pale look of too much work, too little food, and too little happiness.

"What are we going to do?" I asked.

"We must be strong. We'll work as hard as we can. We'll pray that things will get better. We'll love our family and friends. We'll learn to forgive the English who have been cruel to us. That's all we can do."

Every day before we went home after work, Papa, Michel, and I looked for Grand'maman, Grand-père, and Antoine and Emilie's parents, M. and Mme Comeau. One evening we nearly bumped into M. Martin, who was hurrying toward us. "I just met a family that used to live near Grand Pré," he said. "When they got off the ship in another town in Maryland, they walked around for days looking for a place to live. They had to huddle together in the snow at night until a minister finally found a home for them."

I could hardly breathe thinking of their misery. I was freezing, and the wind made me shiver. But I felt guilty for complaining about the little we had, when we had much more than some of our people. We would have shared everything we owned if we had known they needed help.

"Why are you out so late?" asked M. Martin.

"We're still looking for my maman, papa, and M. and Mme Comeau," said Papa. "We look for them every day after work."

"Why don't you put a notice in the newspaper and one in the town square? Someone who knows your parents and the Comeaus might know how to read, and tell them where you are. I'll come to your house later and write the notices for you."

"Come with us now and eat some of Marguerite's delicious soup. Then you can write."

After work a few days later, Papa said, "Pierre, you and Michel collect our food from the farmer. Maman is probably waiting for it. I'll walk around for a while."

The warmth of the fire, the smell of Maman's soup, and happy voices greeted us when we walked into the shed that was our home. Later, the door opened, and Papa stood there with a big smile on his face. "I have a wonderful surprise."

"What is it, Papa?" I hadn't seen him smile in a long time.

"Let me come in out of the cold, and I'll show you." We crowded around the door. Then Grand'maman and Grand-père walked in. Everyone hugged, cried, and talked at once. Pale and thin, Grand'maman looked very tired, but a smile lit up her sweet face.

I put two chairs close to the fire. "Come; sit here where it's warm."

Maman heated soup over the fire in the fireplace. "What happened? Where have you been? We were so worried about you."

"When we got off the boat, we were pushed away from you by the crowd; then we couldn't find you," said Grand-père. "I shouted until I was hoarse, but you were too far away to hear us over the noise of so many people. A priest found a family who gave us a room in their house. They were kind to us, but we wanted to be with you. This afternoon the priest came to tell us he saw your notice in the newspaper. He told us where to find you."

I couldn't stop smiling. Suddenly, our shed seemed brighter and warmer, and was a happier place than it had been before they walked in.

The fire and a bowl of hot soup warmed Grand'maman and Grand-père. But I was shocked at how much older Grand'maman looked in the weeks we were apart.

Maman made soup whenever she had a few vegetables, but Grand'maman ate little, and often said she couldn't get warm.

Since we didn't have enough benches for everyone to sit together to eat, Grand-père asked us to find some wood for him. He borrowed tools from Mme Ange and made another bench and some chairs. He made a rocking chair for Grand'maman and one for Maman. Then he made a chest for Mme Ange to store her clothes. He smiled as he worked and seemed happy to be able to help.

One evening soon after Grand'maman and Grand-père came back to us, a man and a lady knocked at the door. They looked familiar, but I couldn't remember who they were. Emilie and Antoine shouted and ran to them. They all hugged and cried. Their parents!

Tears ran down M. Comeau's cheeks. "We knew one ship stayed here in Annapolis, and we thought it was the one Emilie and Antoine were on. We hoped and prayed they were living with a kind family, and you'd still be here. Our ship brought us to a town about thirty miles south of Annapolis. We couldn't stay there. We couldn't rest until we found our children. We left as soon as we could slip away.

"We walked for miles every day, searching and asking everyone we met if they had seen our children. We happened to meet a friend from Acadie who asked us to stay with his family. By the grace of God, his neighbor saw your notice in the town square. Thank you for taking such good care of our little ones. I can see they've been happy. We'll never be able to repay you for your kindness."

Mme Comeau couldn't say anything. She just cried and hugged Emilie and Antoine as if she would never let them go.

"You would have done the same for us if our children had been lost," said Papa. "Emilie and Antoine are good children. We'll miss them."

They hugged us, and then they were gone. I was happy for their family but very sad for myself. I felt empty inside. I already missed them, especially Antoine. He was always with me when I was at home. I would miss his hand holding mine, and his big brown eyes looking up at me.

Weeks passed, then months. Papa, Michel, and I worked from dawn to dusk every day except Sunday. Poor Papa. He looked so tired. He had owned his own farm since he and Maman got married. It was hard for him to work for someone else. We had never worked so hard for so little.

Maman cooked, cleaned, took care of the children, and begged for clothes and shoes until we each had one set of warm clothes. The ones we wore when we left Grand Pré were thin and tattered and could only be used for rags.

Since we had some fruit, vegetables, and meat to eat, we began to look a little less pale—all except Grand'maman. She seemed to get weaker and paler. In Acadie, she had always been busy cooking, cleaning, and working in her garden. In Maryland, she sat in her rocking chair near the fireplace, a blanket on her legs and one around her shoulders. She peeled and chopped vegetables and did other small chores. I was worried. And seeing the sad looks on the faces of Grand-père, Maman, and Papa when they looked at her, I knew they were worried too.

I was always tired. Even though we had food, there never seemed to be enough for everyone. I didn't have my strength back from our long sea voyage. It was hard working on a farm that wasn't ours. I missed our animals. I wanted to pick fruit and vegetables whenever I was hungry. I wanted to talk to Jean and daydream with him. I wanted my happy life back.

20

Faith

One evening when the snow was finally beginning to melt, there was a knock at the door. M. Martin stood there shivering. "I have news. The governor and legislators have made decisions that concern us. Several Acadians were sent to jail because they were begging for food. They had been looking for work every day but no one would hire them. Their children were taken away from them. The poor children are now working for English families and are being treated like slaves."

Maman took a loaf of bread out of the brick oven built into one side of the fireplace. "Our children could be taken away from us? *Ça c'est terrible.* (That's terrible.) What are we going to do?"

A shiver ran down my spine. What would happen next? Would our lives continue to get worse and worse?

Papa sighed. "I'm thankful that Pierre, Michel, and I have jobs, but we can't trust the English. Many children have been taken from Acadian families. I heard that our people won't be allowed to travel more than ten miles from home without permission. We'll live like prisoners."

"What is even worse, the legislators will decide on the number of Acadians who will be allowed to live in each county in Maryland," said M. Martin. "If there are too many in one area, some will be moved to another place."

"Then we'll never be at peace, knowing they could make us move again at any time, and our children could be taken from us."

"This isn't a good place to live. Many of our people are dying. They're weak from lack of good food and housing, so they can't fight sickness."

Papa paced back and forth. "We can't stay here. I want my own farm so I can grow food for my family. We can't survive on what we are given by the owner of the farm where the boys and I work. I want a good life for my family again. We'll never have that here. We can't take the chance that our children will be taken away from us."

"But where can we go?" asked Maman. "Back to Acadie?"

When she heard the word Acadie, tears began to flow down Grand'maman's cheeks.

"If the French win the war, they'll govern Acadie again," said M. Martin. "Then we'll go back."

Papa sighed. "But if the English win, we'll never go back."

I slumped against the wall where I was sitting. My mouth was dry, and the ache in my stomach seemed to grow larger and larger.

One day blended into the next. I was hardly aware of passing time. I just kept trudging along, doing my work and helping Papa with the farmer's crops when my work was done. Michel and I did as much as we could to help Papa put food on the table. We awoke every morning before dawn, ate our meager breakfast, and then worked until it was too dark to tell the difference between plants and weeds.

Sometimes I thought about how happy we used to be, and I wondered if we would ever be happy again. But usually I was too tired to think. Without our faith in God and our desire for a better life, we wouldn't have been able to keep putting one foot in front of the other, day after day.

21

Hope

Years passed. Jacques, who was only four years old when we left Acadie, worked with Papa, Michel, and me. Brigette and Anne were learning to cook. Elizabeth, no longer a baby, worked in the garden and would soon help in the kitchen.

M. Martin visited whenever he had news. In 1760 he announced, "The men imprisoned in Halifax were brought to Grand Pré and Annapolis Royal to care for the dikes. English farmers now own all the land in Acadie. They don't know anything about dikes and can't farm the land without the Acadian prisoners."

"It must be strange for our people to be back in Grand Pré working for someone else, taking care of the dikes we built," said Papa.

More years dragged by. It was 1763; we had been in Maryland for seven and a half years, and I was nineteen years old. One evening, M. Martin knocked on the door, greeting us with a big smile. "I just heard the best news. England and France signed a peace treaty several months ago, in February. Acadians who were in prison in England were sent to France. The treaty gave all Acadians eighteen months to leave English-owned lands."

"Does that mean we'll be allowed to leave Maryland?" asked Papa.

"I think so. I'll write to the French authorities to find out when ships will arrive to bring us to France."

A few months later, M. Martin, with a sigh, told us, "The peace treaty allowed only Acadians in England to move to lands controlled by the French. It doesn't apply to those of us living in America."

Papa's shoulders drooped. "That means we'll have to spend the rest of our lives here. Nothing has changed."

"And my life will never change," I grumbled softly. "I'll never have a home and a family of my own."

Another evening M. Martin told us, "The English government announced if we take the oath of allegiance to the king of England, we'll be allowed to live wherever we want in English-owned lands. If we don't take the oath, they'll allow us to move to French-owned land, but we'll have to pay our own way. We'll meet in the town square tomorrow evening to discuss what we should do."

The room suddenly seemed brighter. Everyone smiled, and my smile was the biggest of all. "Papa, will we go back to Acadie?"

"I don't know, son. Wait until the meeting tomorrow."

I didn't think I could live that long without knowing what we were going to do. I hardly slept that night, and my mind wasn't on work the next day.

A large group of Acadians gathered in the town square, laughing and talking. Tears welled up in my eyes because I couldn't remember the last time I had heard Acadians laughing. It was beautiful—the sound of hope.

"We'll be allowed to move to French-controlled lands," said Joseph Landry, a relative of our friend François Landry. "But the English now control all of Acadie and all of Canada except for a few islands in the Gulf of St. Lawrence."

"Where can we go?" asked M. Thibodeau.

"The governor of Saint Domingue in the French West Indies has offered to pay for our passage to his country. He needs many people to work on the sugar plantations."

"Where is Saint Domingue?" asked M. Comeau.

"It's an extremely hot island far south of us that is controlled by the French," said M. Landry. "We wouldn't own our land but would work for the owner of a plantation."

Papa walked to the front of the group. "I don't want to work for someone else. I want my own farm. We know what we have here. Life could be much worse for us in Saint Domingue."

"We can't go there," said M. Martin. "We must find another place where we can own land and begin again." Everyone nodded.

"Does anyone have money to pay for passage when we decide where to go?"

"No" was everyone's answer.

"We can stay here if we sign an oath of allegiance to the king of England."

"*No! Never!*" everyone shouted.

"We can ask the governor of Maryland to send us back to Acadie, even though it's ruled by the English," said M. Landry. "Or we could go to another part of Canada where many French people live."

We all agreed that would be better than going to Saint Domingue.

Weeks later, we met again to hear M. Landry's news. "The governor of Maryland wanted to be sure we would be accepted in land controlled by the English before considering our request to pay for our passage. But the English governors don't want us in Acadie or Canada."

"Then where can we go?" asked M. Thibodeau.

"I don't know," said M. Landry. "We could go to *Louisiane* (Louisiana) if we could find a way to get there. Before the peace treaty, France turned Louisiane over to Spain, since the Spanish helped France in the war against England. I don't know if our lives would be better there, but many French people have lived there for years."

"Where is Louisiane?" asked Papa.

"Far to the south. We would have to go by ship."

"How? We don't have any money."

"We'll have to find a way."

"How will the Spanish officers treat us if we go there?"

"We'll wait to see if other Acadians move to Louisiane. We'll meet again when we know more."

Once again, my stomach seemed to turn upside down. I didn't like not knowing what was going to happen to us.

We continued to receive news from our people in other parts of North America. Acadians who could read and write sent letters by travelers on sailing ships. Either M. Martin or M. Landry brought the news to us.

The following year, 1764, several hundred Acadians living in Georgia and South Carolina sailed to Saint Domingue. Later that year, many of our people from Pennsylvania, New York, Connecticut, and Massachusetts joined them.

M. Martin's big smile told us the news was good. "They were welcomed by the French people on the island."

"Maybe we should go to Saint Domingue, too," I said.

"We'll wait for more news before making such a big decision," said Papa.

One day toward the end of the year, M. Martin dragged to our door after work. His head drooped and his shoulders slumped. "What's wrong?" asked Papa.

"A third of our people who went to Saint Domingue already died from yellow fever or malaria."

My whole body felt heavy. I wondered how many of our friends and relatives had moved there, thinking their lives would be better.

And now, those who were still alive were probably suffering more than we were.

In 1765 Joseph Broussard, an Acadian just released from prison in Halifax, led a large group of his people to Saint Domingue. From there, they sailed to New Orleans, a town in Louisiane on the banks of the Mississippi River.

Friends and relatives who reached Louisiane wrote that many people from France had lived happily there since the French founded Louisiane in 1718. The recently arrived Acadians already owned land and were getting settled. Some lived on grasslands and raised cattle. Others had large farms where they raised grain, fruit, and vegetables. They urged us to join them.

In the spring of 1766, I was twenty-two years old. If the English had not disrupted our lives nearly eleven years before, I probably would have been married with a farm of my own. But how could I get married when I couldn't support a wife and family? I owned nothing except the clothes on my back. Papa and Grand-père didn't own any more than I did. We still lived in the shed in Mme Ange's yard. We still worked for the farmer who paid us with food. And I was too tired to even *think* about courting a young lady.

Nothing changed. We worked until we were exhausted. We prayed that someday we would have a better life. That aching feeling of sadness in the pit of my stomach never went away. We couldn't change our lives without help. But who, besides Mme Ange, was willing to help us? Sometimes anger welled up inside me. I had to pray for the feeling to go away, because anger changed nothing.

22

Making Plans

"What a day!" I wiped my sweaty forehead and sighed as Papa, Michel, Jacques, and I trudged home from work one evening in June. I could hardly put one foot in front of the other. "I'm not looking forward to another long, hot summer."

Hearing footsteps, I looked up. M. Martin rushed toward us, shouting, "I have news, great news!"

Papa hurried toward him. "What is it?"

"M. Landry told me that the governor and legislators of Maryland decided to help us get to Louisiane. Even though the eighteen months we were given to leave in 1763 have long passed, they want us to go. They can't wait to get rid of us. They'll even pay part of our passage on a sailing ship. A schooner carrying Acadians from other parts of Maryland will be here next week, on its way to Louisiane. There will be room for us. We must collect money to pay our share. We'll meet at the town square tomorrow after supper."

Papa made the sign of the cross. "Thank God. That is wonderful news."

I smiled, and then frowned. "Papa, do you think the Spanish authorities will treat us better than the English do? Do you think this will be a mistake like it was for the people who went to Saint Domingue?"

"I don't know, Pierre. We can only pray—then wait to see what happens. But if we want to be free to raise our families, worship God, own our own farms, and be happy, we must go. We have no other choice."

A large crowd of Acadians gathered the next evening. As soon as M. Landry held up his hand, everyone stopped talking. "The governor and legislators will help us, but we have to pay for part of our passage on the sailing ship."

"How can we do that, with no money?" asked M. Comeau.

"We'll sell everything except the clothes we're wearing. If you brought anything from Acadie, sell it—anything you can live without. We'll meet again in two days to count the money we have."

Papa's shoulders sagged when he told the family what had been decided. "We don't have anything to sell," he said.

No one said a word. We just sat and stared at the floor. We'd have to stay in Maryland.

But Grand-père stood up and hobbled to the chest where he and Grand'maman kept their clothes. He pulled out something wrapped in a handkerchief and handed it to Papa. My jaw dropped when I saw what it was.

Papa stared at the money. "Where did you get this?"

"Mme Ange showed her friends the chest I made for her to store her clothes. Several of them wanted some of my furniture. While you and the boys were working, I've been making beds, tables, chairs, benches, and chests. I also carved animals for their children. I've been saving the money I earned, hoping that someday we could buy a small piece of land to build a house. I wanted to surprise you, so Mme Ange let me work in her barn. But you must use the money to sail to Louisiane. It isn't much, but it may be enough for your share. We can also sell the furniture I made for us."

We all smiled, laughed, and hugged each other. Anne and Elizabeth danced around the room, even though their only memories were of our life in Maryland.

"Will Louisiane be like Acadie, Maman?" asked Elizabeth, probably remembering the many stories we told about happier times.

"I hope so, my sweet child. I hope you will finally know what it's like to be happy."

"Long before we left Acadie, I heard about Louisiane," said Grand-père. "Traders said that people who are willing to work have a good life there. The weather is warm, and the land is rich and fertile. And you'll be allowed to keep your language and religion."

Papa looked at Grand'maman and Grand-père. "I want you to come with us. I can't leave you here. I know it will be a long, hard trip, but we have to go for the sake of the children."

Grand-père shook his head, "I don't think Grand'maman can make such a long trip. But you must go, even if we don't go with you."

My heart sank. How could we leave Grand'maman and Grand-père? They had been an important part of my life for as long as I could remember. When we lived in Acadie, I went to their house every day, or they came to ours. How could I live without them? We would never see them again if they didn't come with us.

Grand'maman spoke for the first time since hearing the news. "You must go. I want you to be happy and healthy again. I think we should go with you. If we don't, I'm afraid you might decide to stay here because of us. We can't do that to you and the children. The trip will be hard for me, but if I make it, I'll have a chance to get strong and healthy again. If I die on the way, I'll die happy because I'll be with my family."

Grand-père smiled and nodded in agreement.

Talking, smiling people met at the town square two nights later. Everyone had sold something and had a small amount of money to contribute to the group. After he counted it, M. Landry said, "This should be enough. We'll sail in a few days."

So it was settled. Once again, my stomach started turning flip-flops. I was happy and sad at the same time. Our lives might be better and happier again. Grand'maman and Grand-père were coming with us. But we would be traveling farther and farther away from our home in Acadie. We didn't know what life would be like in Louisiane. We didn't know how the Spanish officers would treat us. Would our lives ever get better, or would everything continue to get worse? There was no way to know.

23

Traveling Farther from Home

Three days later, Papa stopped to talk to M. Martin after work, and then hurried home. "Our ship has arrived. We'll sail tomorrow morning. I told the farmer we're leaving. Now I'm going to thank Mme Ange for everything she has done for us."

Mme Ange, carrying some dried fish, came back with Papa. "I hate to see you leave," she said. "You've been very helpful to me."

"You've been a good friend," said Maman. "We wouldn't have survived without your help. We'll miss you."

"Take this fish to eat on the ship. I wish I had more to give you. You're good people." She hugged us all, and then hurried away.

I already missed Mme Ange. I thought of her as another grand'maman. And her small, damp shed had been our home for nearly eleven years.

Papa called us very early the next morning, even earlier than we always woke up to go to work. "Hurry; wake up. It's time to go."

We each gathered quilts and our extra clothes. Maman wrapped a loaf of bread, a few pieces of fruit, and Mme Ange's fish in her apron, and we were ready to leave. Everything else in the little shed belonged to Mme Ange.

We slipped through town in the darkness, until we reached the first building we had stayed in when we arrived in Maryland in 1755. People squeezed in, looking for friends and relatives. Everyone had been so busy trying to survive in Maryland, we'd had little time to visit and enjoy life.

Even though I could hardly keep my eyes open, when I saw the people who were waiting to board the ship, I wanted to dance for joy. We'd be traveling with many of our good friends from Grand Pré. But when I looked around at the families gathered in the big building, I realized there were many missing faces. Those hardy, strong people had not been able to survive the long years of hardship and cruel treatment by the English.

Isadore's father, M. Daigle, and Mme Boudrot hadn't found their families, even though they had never stopped looking. "My wife, our daughters, and our older sons were put on different ships when we left Grand Pré," said M. Daigle. "When Isadore and I arrived in Maryland, we walked miles and miles looking for them, sleeping in barns along the way. We put notices in the newspaper and in the town square. We asked everyone we saw, but we couldn't find any of our family. I'll never stop looking—I pray I'll find them someday. They could have been sent to one of the other American colonies, or they may already be in Louisiane."

Our large group prayed together before we boarded the ship. We prayed for our safety, and that of our relatives and friends. We asked God for a better life in Louisiane.

As we walked toward the ship, I thought of the first time I boarded a ship on that terrible day in October 1755. Soldiers, with their guns and bayonets, barked orders. Tears streamed down the faces of women and children. Men begged, and women and children screamed when families were separated. Broken furniture and dishes were strewn as far as I could see. Sadness was everywhere.

Now, in the summer of 1766, people laughed and talked. There were no soldiers around, only sailors preparing to cast off. There were no tears. We didn't mourn possessions we had to leave because we owned almost nothing.

When we left Acadie, we looked back and yearned for our happy, pleasant lives. Leaving Maryland, we looked forward to our new lives. We hoped to see relatives and friends we hadn't seen for almost eleven years. The Acadians had sent many letters urging us to join them in Louisiane. "The weather is hot," they said. "The work is endless, but we own our land. We are free. We can speak French without worrying about English soldiers hearing us. We pray. We enjoy life."

The captain greeted us when we boarded the ship. "Welcome. We'll have a good trip."

"How many people are sailing?" asked Papa.

"Two hundred twenty-four people, all anxious to live in Louisiane. A large number of Acadians living in Maryland and Pennsylvania are making plans to follow you as soon as they can arrange for ships to take them."

Our happiness increased as we greeted many of our friends who had been living in other towns in Maryland and were already on the ship. The captain told us we would stop at several other ports in Maryland to pick up more Acadians. We talked about the years since we left Grand Pré and about our hopes for the future.

I stood on deck as we sailed from Annapolis into Chesapeake Bay, then into the Atlantic Ocean. My only sadness was leaving Mme Ange. But suddenly, with a sinking feeling, I realized I would never return to Acadie, the place where I had been so happy.

The trip was long, and we were crowded. But this time we weren't prisoners. We were allowed to stand on deck as long and as often as we wanted. We could visit with the other Acadians. Grand'maman was pale and weak; she rarely climbed the steep ladder to leave our sleeping quarters. We worried about her, but whenever someone asked her how she felt, she always said, "Don't worry about me. I'm right where I want to be, with my family and friends."

I spent most of my waking hours on deck, watching the land whenever we could see it in the distance as we sailed past.

I enjoyed the breeze that ruffled my hair and the salty smell of the sea. I felt free. I liked to watch the sailors as they worked. For the first time in years, I thought of the plans my cousin Jean and I had made when we were eleven years old. We had wanted great adventures. When Jean left Grand Pré with his family, we promised we would sail together some day. Did I still want to sail? Or did I want to be a farmer? I didn't know.

When our dried fish and fruit were gone, we ate the salt pork and hard, dry bread the sailors gave us. I was sick of that in just a few days. I wanted to smell and taste some of Maman's good soup.

One day Grand-père and I were on deck together, watching the sea gulls. "Grand-père, do you think we'll find more of our friends and relatives when we get to Louisiane?"

"If God is willing. We don't know where the English commander sent the other Acadians. We do know a large number of them are now living in Louisiane. We must be thankful we're together again with so many of our people who were in other parts of Maryland. We can only hope and pray that many more of our friends and relatives are in Louisiane."

Part Five
Louisiana
1766-69

ENGLISH TERRITORY

Baton Rouge

Lake Maurepas

Lake Pontchartrain

Acadian Coast

German Coast

New Orleans

LOUISIANA

SPANISH TERRITORY

Mississippi

River

GULF OF MEXICO

GULF OF MEXICO

ACADIAN

COAST

1766

24

Louisiana, not Louisiane

The weather was already hot when we left Maryland, but I soon
realized I didn't know how miserable summer heat could be. The
farther south we traveled, the hotter and more humid it was. "I hate
this burning sun," I grumbled one day, wiping my face. "I've never
been so uncomfortable before. Will the weather in Louisiane be like
this? I want some snow."

"Pierre," said Papa softly. "I wish we could go back to Acadie, but
we can't. I think we'll be happy with French-speaking people who,
like us, are Catholics. We have to go to Louisiane."

"I'm sorry, Papa," I said. "I know you're right. I'll have to learn
to live with the heat."

The captain walked over to us, pointing. "That's the Mississippi
River. We're ready to go upriver to New Orleans."

"How long will that take?" I asked.

"We'll need strong winds to move our ship against the current
in the river. We could be there in less than a week if everything is in
our favor. But at times we've had to dock on the side of the river for
days, waiting for the wind to blow in the right direction."

As we sailed up the Mississippi River to New Orleans, my friends and family spent our days on deck, talking about the future. My heart beat faster when I thought about owning land again. Someday I might even have a house of my own, and maybe a wife and children. Life would be better here.

The wind was favorable, and I was on deck the morning the captain announced, "We're very close to New Orleans. We should be there in less than an hour."

I looked around at the Acadians who were anxiously waiting to begin again in this new land. Even though we were excited, everyone looked worn and pale. For eleven years in Maryland, food had been scarce and work was never-ending. Three months on a crowded ship with little exercise and a steady diet of dried fish, dried meat, and hard bread had not improved our health. It seemed remarkable that only fourteen people had died during the voyage. Before getting off the ship, we gathered to thank God for bringing us safely to Louisiane.

Two French officers met us and led us into a large building. "*Soyez le bienvenu*! (Welcome!) We're happy you've come here to live. Louisiane has been transferred to the Spanish government; they renamed it Louisiana. Since the Spanish officers haven't taken control yet, we'll help you get settled. You'll rest here for a week or so, and then one of us will take one or two people from each family farther up the Mississippi River to the area where you will live. You'll be given land grants."

"All of us?" I asked.

"Yes, the French government has been giving land along the river to your people, and the Spanish leaders have agreed to do the same. In return, you'll clear the land near the water, build a house, and plant enough crops to support your family. If you do that within three years, it will all be yours."

"Do any Acadians live in the area where we're going?" asked M. Martin.

"Yes, they have begun to settle there."

I wanted to shout for joy. This sounded like the perfect way to begin our new life. And when I saw bread, cheese, and fruit laid out on a table for us, I thought life couldn't get any better. But a few hours later, it did get better. The soldiers returned with some beef and vegetables that their wives had cooked. What a treat that was!

We spent the next two weeks resting, eating, and walking around the city with its narrow streets and wooden sidewalks. Mosquitoes were annoying, but I enjoyed the evening sounds of crickets and frogs.

One afternoon, one of the French officers walked into the building where we were staying. "The men who are going upriver first will leave at dawn tomorrow. Another ship will sail a day or two later to bring everyone else. Those of you who are staying here may walk around as much as you like until you join your husbands."

"I'd like to go with you tomorrow," I said.

"Me, too," said Isadore.

"There should be enough room," said the officer.

M. Martin said, "I'll choose a small piece of land for you, Mme Hébert, and for you, Mme Boudrot, if you want me to."

"Yes, please do," said Mme Hébert.

"Merci," said Mme Boudrot. "I just need enough room for a small house, a few fruit trees, a small vegetable garden, and a few chickens."

I didn't sleep well that night because I couldn't stop thinking. This was the place where we were going to live. But would it finally be the place where we *wanted* to live?

25

Land Grants

The sky was clear and the air was unexpectedly pleasant for our trip upriver the next day. The river wandered between woods on both shores. Near evening, we passed a settlement with many houses and farms. "Is this where we're going to live?"

"No," said the officer. "This is called the German Coast because many German farmers live here. They grow much of the food used by the people who live in New Orleans. We're going farther upriver to the next settlement. It's an area people have started to call the Acadian Coast. We'll be there tomorrow."

The smell of flowers and ripe fruit on the trees, along with the clean, neat farms and houses, gave me a warm, pleasant feeling deep inside. It reminded me of Acadie.

I pointed to the trees along the shore. "What's that stringy, gray stuff hanging from the trees?"

"That is moss. We call it Spanish moss because it reminds us of the Spaniards' beards. We use it to stuff mattresses, pillows, and cushions for furniture. It hangs on the branches of trees, but it doesn't hurt them because it gets its nourishment from the air."

I was on deck the next day when we rounded a bend in the river and saw houses and farms.

"Look!" Everyone on deck shouted at the same time.

The officer pointed to a wooded area past the farms. "This land could be for any one of you. Each family's land starts at the riverbank and extends back forty arpents."

"The French measurement is used here?" I asked.

"Yes, since Louisiana was originally owned by France. As you probably know, an arpent equals 192 feet. A land grant of forty arpents is almost a mile and a half deep. The width is usually between three and six arpents, depending on the size of your family."

"That's a lot of land," said M. Martin.

"The land near the water can be cleared for your house, a barn, and a place to grow crops," the officer continued. "This soil is rich and fertile. Your crops will be healthy and strong. Farther back, the land doesn't drain as well, so it isn't good for crops. But it's perfect for farm animals; they find food in the underbrush. Behind that is swampland—the best place to hunt for wild animals. They can be used for food, and their fur can be used for trade. This can all be yours if you're willing to work."

"We'll work hard," Papa said as everyone nodded.

As the boat moved nearer the shore, we heard a shout. A man standing on the bank of the river waved, and then spoke to us. In French! I thought I must be dreaming *"Où allez-vous?"* (Where are you going?) Maybe I wasn't dreaming.

Getting out of the boat, M. Martin spoke for the group. "We're looking for a place to live."

"Je m'appelle Henri Richard. (My name is Henri Richard.) Where are you from?"

"We lived in Acadie, which is now called Nova Scotia. We were sent away by the English lieutenant-governor in September 1755. We lived in Maryland until we were able to get passage on a sailing ship.

We hope to start a new life here. We are farmers." He introduced everyone in our group to M. Richard.

"You're in the right place," said M. Richard. "I'm delighted you're here. I'm also from Acadie, near Port Royal. My family was among the first Acadians who settled in Louisiana, in April 1764. We came from New York, where we had lived since we were deported from Acadie in 1755."

"Are you happy here?"

"Oh, yes. We miss our family and friends, but we have a good life. It's much better than always worrying about what the English soldiers will do to us. We're at peace. There are several other families from Acadie who arrived recently. Later, we'll all get together to talk more."

M. Martin looked around. "This is wild, overgrown land."

"Yes, it is." M. Richard pointed to the closest farm. "But look at my land over there. It was as wild as this when I came here almost two and a half years ago. My sons and I worked hard, cutting down trees, planting crops, and building our house. It was exhausting work, but it was worth it. My neighbors helped us more than I can ever repay."

"You've done a lot in two years," said Papa.

"I have much more work to do. I'm growing enough crops now to feed my family. But next year, I want to plant additional crops so I can trade some for animals. I want another cow, a few pigs, and more chickens. As soon as I have time, I'll build a bigger barn, and someday, a bigger house."

M. Comeau looked around but didn't move. "There's underbrush and so many trees, bushes, and vines. How will we ever clear the land for a house and crops?"

I was happy he said what I'd been thinking.

"You'll have to work hard, and it will take many long months. But we'll help you as much as we can," said M. Richard. "Remember, I haven't been here quite two and a half years. Look at my land now. And look at how my crops are thriving."

M. Martin said, "We want to work. We want to feed our families good food so they'll grow strong and healthy again."

I looked at M. Richard's farm. "Papa, we'll have our own land again."

"Yes, son. Our own land."

M. Richard started to walk back to his farm; then he turned around. "Come eat with us after you have chosen your land. I'll tell my wife. And watch out for snakes and alligators."

"We had snakes in Acadie. But what are alligators?" everyone asked at the same time. M. Richard was already gone.

26

New Friends

"I'll tell you if I see any alligators," said the French officer. "Then you'll know what to look for. They're usually in or near the water."

Each man, carefully watching where he walked, chose the land he wanted. Papa wanted the section where we were standing, next to M. Richard's farmland.

Isadore dashed back shouting, "Pierre, my papa wants the land next to yours."

"Great!"

Then M. Comeau came back, smiling. "We'll take the land on the other side of M. Daigle; Mme Hébert and Mme Boudrot can have the next two sections."

I had a nice warm feeling inside. I would be able to see my friends often. All of the other men who traveled from Maryland with us had chosen land close by.

"Where will we live until we can clear the land and build our homes?" asked M. Comeau.

"You should build a small temporary house now and start planting vegetables," said the French officer. "Then you must each build a levee along the river to protect your land. In the spring, the water in the river sometimes gets so high it overflows. You don't want it to wash your house and crops away. You must also make a road, wide enough for a wagon, next to the levee."

"Is a levee what we call a dike in Acadie?" asked Papa.

"Yes," said the officer.

Papa smiled. "Then we know all about building levees."

"We want you to begin right away to improve your land and plant crops so you can feed your families. Let's go back to the boat so we can get your supplies."

M. Martin stopped walking and turned to the officer. "Supplies?"

"We'll help you get started in your new life. I'll introduce you to Louis Judice, one of the early settlers. Since he lives here, he has some of the things you'll need at his house. He'll do whatever he can to help you."

The officer brought us to the small house where M. Judice lived. They gave each family seeds, a shotgun and ammunition, and the tools we would need—an ax, a sickle, a hoe, and a spade. They also gave us corn, dried meat, a smoked ham, a basket full of vegetables, and a basket of fruit. The spicy, smoky smell of the ham and the sweet smell of the fruit made me hungry.

As each man accepted his supplies, I looked at Papa. A smile lit his face, and I wondered if he was thinking the same thing I was. English soldiers had seized our guns and ammunition, and now a French officer was giving us guns, ammunition, and much more. Maybe this *was* the place where we wanted to live.

As the officer helped us put the supplies in the boat, he said, "Don't forget to come back for your animals once you are settled."

"Animals?" I said.

"Yes, the French government will help you until you harvest your first crops. Each family will be given six hens, a rooster, a cow, and a calf."

M. Martin had a big smile on his face. "This is much more than we hoped for."

We went back to M. Richard's house with the officer. It was peaceful sitting in the shade of the big trees in his yard. When she heard our voices, Mme Richard hurried out to greet us. "You must be tired and hungry. Supper is almost ready." The smell of meat and vegetables drifting through the open windows made my mouth water.

It had been many years since I had seen Papa looking so happy. "It's hard to believe someone would give us so much just to make our homes here," he said. "Our wives won't believe it."

I was there, and I couldn't believe it. These people wanted us to live in Louisiana and were going to help us get started! I felt warm all over, and it wasn't because of the Louisiana heat.

"We want you here," said M. Richard. "We'll help you. But you'll have to work very hard."

"We know how to work hard," said Papa.

A little more of the sadness and emptiness inside me was pushed aside. In their place were a tiny glimmer of hope and a little feeling of warmth. Maybe we would be happy again someday.

When Mme Richard rang the supper bell, two young men came in from the fields. The older one, named Claude, was about my age. The other was about Michel's age. Two younger girls helped their mother in the kitchen. I hoped we would all be friends.

Several of M. Richard's neighbors came to meet us, bringing as much food as they could carry. They were all from Acadie. Jean Baptiste and Jules Terriot appeared to be about my age.

Everyone welcomed us. They wanted to know about our lives since we left Acadie, and we wanted to hear about theirs. We talked until we were hoarse.

"There's room for everyone to sleep in our barns," said M. Richard. "I'm sorry our houses aren't big enough for everyone, but you'll be comfortable. Someday soon I hope my boys and I will have time to build a permanent home."

"Another one?" asked Papa.

"Yes. Our first home was a hut like the one we'll help you build; then last year we built the house we're living in now. Someday, I want a more comfortable one—similar to many of the houses in New Orleans—two rooms wide, raised above the ground with a wood floor and more windows than we have now. I'd also like a loft upstairs for the boys and a porch where we can enjoy the cool breezes. Most of the Acadians here want the same kind of house, but I'm afraid it will be a few years before any of us will have time for so much work. We have enough to do now putting food on the table, taking care of our animals, and trying to grow extra food to sell."

Even though we enjoyed the food and the company, it had been a long, tiring day, so we soon headed for our beds in the barn.

Before we left Acadie, I wouldn't have believed sleeping in a barn would have made me so happy. But it was a roof over our heads, and there was Spanish moss for soft beds for all of us. I was with Papa and my friends from Acadie. I had new friends who spoke French. We had land where we would build a house and grow crops. I slept better than I had in months.

27

Helpful Neighbors

Our rest was over. We had work to do, and we were excited and anxious to get started.

Carrying our tools, Papa and I hurried to our land the next morning after breakfast. But once we were there, I couldn't move.

I looked around and pointed. "Papa, look at this. How are we going to clear this land so we can build a house and plant crops? It's nothing like our farmland in Acadie. We can't do it. Maybe we should have stayed in Maryland."

"We'll do what my great-grandpère did when he sailed to Acadie from France in 1671. Those settlers found nothing but forests and marshland when they arrived. They didn't use the forests for their farms like we're going to do, but they had to build dikes and drain the marshland. They worked as hard to get settled as we'll have to work here. If they could do it, we can. Never forget, Acadians are hard workers who don't give up."

Years before, Grand-père had told me the story about the first settlers in Acadie. That was a story I thought I would remember forever. But I had forgotten because so much had happened since then. It seemed as if our lives had been turned upside down. I had forgotten something else, too. Acadians always help one another.

We started chopping vines and underbrush near the river but stopped when we heard voices. A large group of men and boys appeared. M. Judice, M. Richard and his sons, our friends who sailed from Maryland with us, the neighbors we met the day before at M. Richard's house, and some strangers were all carrying scythes and axes.

M. Richard waved when he saw us. "We're here to help you. Some of these Acadians settled here soon after my family, and others arrived recently. We don't have much work on our own farms right now. We'll help you; then we'll help the rest of the families. It will go much faster if we all work together. We'll start by clearing enough land for a small hut for each family. It won't take long."

By the end of the day, the piles of vines and small bushes on each family's land were as high as my head. The only thing I wanted to do was sink into the Spanish moss in M. Richard's barn and close my eyes. But the tempting smell of meat and vegetables made me realize how hungry I was, and our supper tasted even better than it smelled.

The next morning, as soon as there was enough light for us to see, we were all back at work. We didn't stop until we heard a boat on the river. People waved as the boat pulled to shore. It was the women and children who had stayed in New Orleans and the older men, like Grand-père, who wouldn't have farms of their own. I breathed a prayer of thanks when I saw Grand'maman. She looked rested and wasn't as pale as she'd been on the ship to Louisiana.

After hugs and kisses, we returned to our work until we heard more voices near the river. This time it was Mme Richard accompanied by a large group of women and children, walking from their homes.

"You must be hungry," said one of the ladies.

The women carried baskets and dishes of cooked food. They brought ham, chicken stew, vegetables and fruit, and even some butter and cheese, since the Acadian families had cows. All of the women were soon chatting like old friends as they put the dishes of food on cloths under the trees. When everything was ready, they called us to eat a delicious meal. That gave me time to meet the rest of our neighbors. I looked forward to making many new friends.

I watched the Acadian girls who had been in Louisiana for a year or two, and thought about how pretty they were. My thoughts surprised me. For the last eleven years, I had lived dead-tired, working from dawn to dark six days a week to help Papa put enough food on the table so we could survive one more day. Always too tired to think, I had only hoped and prayed that someday things would be better. The Acadian girls in Maryland were as thin and exhausted as I was—their eyes dead, and their smiles long gone.

The color in the cheeks of the Louisiana Acadians made them look alive. Their bright eyes lit up their faces when they smiled, as they often did. Maybe, just maybe, I might want to court one of them someday. And I hoped that soon my sisters would look just as pretty and healthy again.

Antoine, now fourteen years old, sat on the ground with the older boys and young unmarried men. Since the first time he climbed on my lap when he was three years old, I had thought of him as a younger brother. He pointed to a plate of something cut in squares, yellow in the middle and light brown on the top and bottom. "What's that?"

"Cornbread," said Claude. "Try a piece with lots of butter."

Antoine took a big bite as butter smeared his chin. "Umm, good."

M. Richard sat nearby. "We don't grow wheat here, so we can't make the kind of bread we ate in Acadie. Since corn grows well, we grind it to make cornbread. Taste the watermelon and oranges, too. I'll bet you've never tasted anything so good."

Antoine took a piece of watermelon. Juice dripped down his chin and onto his shirt. "Umm. Sweet and juicy."

"And you're a mess," laughed Claude. "We should throw you in the river for a bath."

"Time to get back to work," said M. Richard when we finished eating. "We're going to start building your houses today. It won't take long, because they'll be small and temporary, like Indian huts. You can live in them until you have time to build something larger. All of us lived in huts until we planted our crops and built our levees and roads."

While the women and children packed the dishes and food, the men and boys cut small willow trees. They worked well together, each knowing what his job was and doing it quickly. They showed us how to build a hut out of small poles standing on end, side by side. We threaded smaller branches through, crossways, to hold the poles together. The roof was made of palmetto fronds. With the men cutting trees and hammering poles into the ground, the boys cutting branches and weaving them through the poles, and the women and bigger girls gathering palmetto fronds for the roof, we soon had a small, comfortable place to live. The younger children worked all afternoon gathering Spanish moss for our beds.

M. Richard stood back and looked at our hut. "This will be all you'll need for now. We'll finish everyone's hut in a few days."

Mme Richard turned to Maman, Mme Comeau, Mme Hébert, Mme Martin, and Mme Boudrot. "If you ladies come to my house when we finish building the huts, I'll teach you how to spin thread from cotton."

"Cotton?" said Maman.

"We all grow enough cotton for our own use. It's cool and comfortable for clothes and sheets in hot weather. I'll show you how to remove the seeds and spin thread, and how to clean and dry Spanish moss. The moss the children picked today can be used for your beds for now. But if you're going to stuff mattresses with it, you must prepare it first."

* * *

We were so busy that the days passed quickly. As soon as everyone had a hut, Papa marked off an area for Maman's vegetable garden. "We'll plant enough now to have the food we need. When we finish building the levee, a bigger house, a barn, and fences, we can plant more crops. In the next few years, we'll cut down more trees to enlarge our farmland. Then we'll trade the crops for animals."

"I wish we had more cows and some pigs," I said. "I miss eating beef and ham."

"So do I," said Papa. "It will just take time."

Mosquitoes were annoying, biting wherever they found uncovered skin, and sometimes even biting through thin clothing. It seemed as if I was always slapping at them, and saying, "Ouch!" when another one bit me.

"What are those?" I asked Claude one day, pointing to some flying insects with delicate-looking wings.

"We call them mosquito hawks because they eat mosquitoes."

"I'm glad something eats mosquitoes so they'll stop trying to eat me. I hate biting insects."

I also hated seeing snakes slither through the underbrush. I always wanted to drop whatever I was doing and run as far as I could, maybe all the way back to Acadie.

I knew I had to look forward to my new life. I had to learn to be happy in this new land, but sometimes I couldn't help looking back, and wishing for the life we had left behind.

28

Taming the Land

It was a blessing that the weather was comfortable because our work seemed endless. I soon found out how hard it was going to be to tame this wild forest and swampland. Our Louisiana neighbors helped us cut down trees in the section Papa had marked off for Maman's garden, but we still had stumps everywhere. Maybe we couldn't have a farm. Maybe Papa had picked the wrong land. But all of the land along the river looked the same.

I gazed around. "How are we going to get rid of the tree stumps? How are we going to plant vegetables? This land is nothing like our farmland in Acadie."

Jean Baptiste grinned at me. "We'll show you how to work, farm boy."

Axes rang through the air as the men and older boys chopped the roots around the smaller tree stumps. When there was nothing more to chop, they dug up the roots that were left.

"I still don't know how we're going to plant a garden with those big tree stumps," I said.

M. Richard put his arm around my shoulders. "I know this looks as if it will never work, but we plant between the big stumps until they rot in the ground. That's the only way we can farm this land."

Many long days passed before we finished helping the other Acadians clear land for their gardens. But finally, everyone had a small plot of land ready for planting.

Walking out the door one morning, Papa said, "Come on, boys; it's time to build a barn. It won't be long before the weather is cold, and our animals will need shelter."

I picked up my hat and followed him. "Jean Baptiste told me he's been here over two years, and it has never snowed."

"I know. It doesn't get nearly as cold here as it does in Acadie, but our animals will still need a warm, dry area."

"I can't imagine a winter without icy, cold weather and lots of snow."

"We'll get used to it, just as we'll get used to the heat in the summer," replied Papa.

A few weeks later, Papa took a deep breath and looked around. "We did it, Pierre. Some of the hardest, heaviest work is finally done. We have a hut to live in and a barn for the animals. The ground is ready for Maman to plant her vegetable garden. But we still have a lot to do. I wish we could build a house now, but I know that's not possible."

"Why do you want to do that now? We have so many other things to do," I said.

"The weather is getting colder, and I'm afraid our little hut will be uncomfortable when the winter winds start blowing. We'll do our best to keep warm. We'll fill the cracks in our hut with mud, and hope we can build our house next year. We'll get through this as we've gotten through difficulties that were a lot worse. Our hut is big enough for all of us. Our family is together, and we're at peace."

29

Everyone Works

The next few months were extremely busy for all of us. Each new family from Maryland needed a bigger house, furniture, barns, crops, clothes, sheets, blankets, and mattresses. We had to build a levee and a road connecting to the neighbors' roads. The list of things everyone needed seemed to go on forever. But, of course, our neighbors helped us just as we helped them.

Even though we couldn't build another house right away, it was always in the back of my mind. Just thinking about everything we had to do made me tired. I didn't have time to think about sailing. At night I fell into the Spanish moss and was asleep as soon as I closed my eyes. I was still tired when I woke up, but I had to go right back to work. There wasn't time for daydreaming.

While we were busy working outside, Maman and the girls had plenty to do inside. Besides cooking, cleaning, and caring for Grand'maman, Maman made another set of clothes for each of us. First, she had to spin thread from cotton on a spindle, weave cloth on the small loom Grand-père made for her, and then make the clothes. She made quilts, sheets, towels, and mattress and pillow covers that we would stuff with moss when we had a house with room for beds.

Mme Hébert, her daughters, and Mme Boudrot helped Maman and my sisters with the spinning and weaving. They also helped Maman and Grand-père plant the seeds in our vegetable garden. "Since your husband and sons are doing so much to help us get settled, we'll help you," said Mme Boudrot. "M. Richard told us to plant cabbage, turnips, and mustard greens now. It will soon be time to plant peas."

"That sounds like the food we grew in Acadie," said Maman.

Somehow, after the vegetable seeds were planted, Maman found time to learn to weave palmetto fronds to make baskets, and hats for us to wear in the summer. Grand'maman was weak, but she helped with this job as much as she could. The girls helped too.

Papa, Michel, Jacques, and I were busy building a dike—I mean a levee—between the front of our property and the river. I have to remember we're in Louisiana, and they are called levees. We built them the same way we built our dikes in Acadie, but we didn't need gates under the levees because the land near the river didn't have to be drained.

The weather was usually pleasant, and sometimes cold, but we didn't mind working outside. The cold felt good after the long, hot summer that we spent in Maryland and on the sailing ship to Louisiana. And we didn't have to trudge through ice and deep snow every time we walked outside, as we did in Acadie. I was happy to finish a good part of the levee before the weather was blisteringly hot again.

When we lived in Grand Pré, Grand-père took care of his large farm with the help of his sons and grandsons. But the month on the sailing ship from Grand Pré to Maryland with little to eat, our years in Maryland, and another long trip to Louisiana had left him too tired, and his legs too weak, to work on our land. He liked to stay close to the house to help Maman take care of Grand'maman. He also helped Maman and the girls plant and harvest the vegetables in the garden.

Grand-père spent the rest of his time making furniture. He made a narrow bed for Grand'maman, a table, two benches, and a small loom for Maman. There wasn't room for anything else in our tiny hut. At night, we pushed the furniture against the walls so we would have room to spread the moss we used for our beds.

As soon as we had finished building our barn, Grand-père started making more furniture.

Watching him one day, I asked, "Where are you going to put that bed? There isn't room for any more furniture in our little hut."

He put his tools down and smiled at me. "I know, Pierre, but I want to keep busy. Since we only have a cow and calf, a pig, and a few chickens, there's enough room to store the furniture in the barn. We can section off one end for the animals. When the new house is built, the furniture will be ready."

So he made beds for everyone, chairs, a bigger table, and chests for storing clothes. Then he made rocking chairs for the adults. The last piece of furniture was for Maman.

"Here's the cradle I promised to make for you, Marguerite," he said. "This is for the grandchildren and great-grandchildren you'll have someday."

"Thank you," she said, with tears in her eyes. "I'll always treasure it. It's even more beautiful than the one I had in Acadie."

"Now I have to keep my promise to Pierre," he said. "I'll do as much as I can to help around the farm and in the garden. But I'll also start whittling animals like the ones I used to make in Acadie. Someday I'll have great-grandchildren who will play with them."

That made me smile.

Seeing Grand-père smile again while he made furniture made my work seem a little easier. But what made me feel even better was hearing Maman sing while she worked. The worried look on her face was gone. She didn't seem to mind the chores or the cramped hut. She was happy again, and that made all of us happier.

30

Planting

Because we were so busy, spring was in the air before we knew it. Pink, yellow, and white wildflowers dotted the levee and perfumed the air with their sweet smell. Bees buzzed, gathering nectar.

We were already enjoying cabbage, turnips, and mustard greens from Maman's garden, but we needed a larger area for crops that we could exchange someday for other things we needed. Several of the neighbors helped us clear another section of land. We cut the smaller trees to burn in the fireplace and put the bigger ones aside. Later they would be cut into the boards we would use to build our house. It wasn't long before the pile of trees was high and wide. I knew we would soon have enough to start building.

Michel looked at the seeds M. Richard brought. "What are we going to plant?"

"Crops you've never planted before, like corn and cotton. They should be planted now." M. Richard turned over a shovelful of dirt. "In a month or two, after we help the neighbors plant their corn and cotton, we'll also plant squash, sweet potatoes, pumpkins, and melons. I know you'll want pear trees, because you grew those in Acadie. You should plant orange, plum, fig, and peach trees, too. Many people grow indigo to make blue dye for their clothes. Spring is a busy time for farmers."

The weather was so pleasant that we enjoyed being outside, even though our work kept us busy from morning to night. Sometimes I wondered if we would ever finish everything that had to be done. But then I gave thanks because the land was ours, and we were at peace at last.

* * *

Unfortunately, much too soon, the summer heat and humidity replaced the delightful spring weather. Since we had arrived in the fall the year before, I didn't know what to expect, but it was hotter than I had ever imagined it could be. I couldn't believe the extreme heat and humidity. It never seemed to get cool; it was even hot and sticky at night. We often lay on our beds of Spanish moss, trying to cool off by fanning ourselves with fans Maman made from palmetto fronds. Unfortunately, we only moved the hot air around.

As Michel, Jacques, Claude, and I started working one morning, I slashed wildly at some weeds. We were helping several of the neighbors finish clearing land for the crops they would plant in the fall. I was already sweating. "This isn't anything like the pleasant weather we had in Acadie."

"You'll get used to it," said Claude. "Then you won't mind it quite as much. We don't usually have this much work in the summer. We just have a lot to do now to help you newly arrived Acadians get settled."

Papa heard me complaining. "If we were in Acadie now, the weather would be comfortable, but we'd be waiting to see what the English would do next."

"I know, Papa. I'm thankful we're here." I started working after wiping my sweaty forehead on my shirtsleeve.

"You're lucky that my maman taught your maman and grand'maman how to make palmetto hats," said Claude. "Without your wide-brimmed hat, your face and neck would be as red as a boiled crab."

I smiled at him, thinking about how everyone was helping to make our lives better. I was happy we didn't have to worry about the English governor and soldiers, but still I missed our home, friends, and neighbors, and especially Jean and his family.

I wanted to do nothing except sit in a shady spot where there was a breeze, trying to keep cool. I was exhausted from the work we had done, and I didn't want to think about everything we still had to do. Many long, hot days passed before we finished, but finally everyone's fall crops were planted.

Sometimes after our chores were done, we had an hour or two to visit with our Louisiana neighbors. One day, as Claude and I relaxed under a tree, he said, "Pierre, I'll have to teach you, Michel, and Isadore how to be Acadians in Louisiana. Living in this swampy land is not like living in Acadie."

I didn't know life could be the same in some ways, yet so different in other ways. I didn't know there would be so much more for us to learn.

31

Strange Creatures

Claude came over one afternoon after he finished his chores. Michel and I were picking moss from our trees, but a lot of it was on branches too high for us to reach.

"What are you doing?" he asked.

"Picking moss. Grand'maman needs a thicker mattress," I said.

He gestured for us to follow him. "It'll take you all year, the way you're doing it. Come with me. I'll show you how to pick moss." We followed him to the swampy area far behind his house.

"What is *that*?" I asked, pointing to a strange-looking dugout canoe sitting on a high, dry spot near the water.

"It's a pirogue. The Indians taught us how to hollow out tree trunks. It's great for getting around in swamps and bayous. I'll show you how to make one another time. I can see I have a lot to teach you. But today we have to gather moss for your grand'maman. Instead of the pirogue, we'll use the other boat. It's wider and won't turn over when we stand up in it to reach the moss. Here, Michel, hold this pole. Be careful—it's long. Pierre and I will put the boat into the water."

The swamp was full of trees dripping with moss—trees so close together that very little sunlight could filter through.

Claude picked up an oar. "I'll paddle. Pierre, use the hook on the end of the pole to pull moss down from the trees. Just don't put your hands into the water. A hungry alligator might think your fingers are his dinner."

"Are there alligators around here?" I asked.

"There's one sunning itself near the edge of the water."

"I thought that was a log."

"You wouldn't think so if it opened its mouth, and you saw its sharp teeth."

A cold shiver ran down my back at the thought of alligators. I wanted to stay far away from them.

It didn't take long to fill the boat with moss. We piled it on dry land, and then went back for more. In a short time we gathered enough to make Grand'maman's mattress more comfortable, and there would be plenty left over for the rest of us.

We walked home, our arms piled high with moss. "You were right, Claude," I said. "That was fast, and fun, too. Thanks for the help."

A few days later, Claude called Isadore, Michel, and me. His arms were filled with large bags. "Come on. I'm going to show you how to catch food for your dinner."

"What kind of food?" I asked.

"You'll see."

"What's inside the bags you're carrying?" asked Isadore. "They look as if they're made of rope."

"I have kernels of corn inside. Let's go to the bayou," he said, pointing to brownish-looking water in the distance.

"Bayou?"

"Boy, the three of you have a lot to learn. You haven't done much exploring yet, have you? A bayou is a very slow-moving stream. There are lots of them around here. I'll make real bayou boys out of all of you in a few years."

As soon as we reached the water, he dipped one of the bags in. When he pulled it out a few minutes later, it was full of strange, gray creatures.

"What are those?" yelled Michel, backing away.

"They are shrimp, and, boy, are they good to eat!"

I shuddered. "They don't look like anything I want to eat."

It wasn't long before all of Claude's bags were filled with shrimp. He picked up several of them. "Come on. Help me bring these home." The four of us walked back to his house, our arms loaded with the heavy bags.

Mme Richard smiled when she saw what we were carrying. "Such big shrimp! Isadore and Pierre, tell your families they must come to our house for supper. Tell the Comeaus, the Martins, Mme Hébert, and Mme Boudrot to come, too. Claude will invite the other neighbors. We'll have a shrimp boil. Probably none of you ever ate shrimp before."

"I never even *saw* shrimp before," I said.

Mme Richard handed one bag of shrimp to Claude. "Please take these out to dry."

"Come on." Claude motioned for us to follow him. He emptied the bag of shrimp onto some boards which were laid out on the ground near the cornfield, away from the trees.

"Why are you doing that?" I asked.

"We're going to let them dry in the sun. Come on; you can help me. We'll take the heads off now. After the shrimp tails are dry, we'll put them in a cloth and shake them, and the shells will fall off. Then we'll pick out the tails and put them away to eat when we don't have fresh shrimp."

I didn't like to touch the strange little creatures, but I helped Claude take off the heads and spread the tails out.

That evening, the neighbors walked to M. Richard's house carrying platters and bowls of food. A delicious smell filled the air as M. Richard boiled the fresh shrimp over a fire in the backyard. They turned pink in the hot water. He spooned some of the steaming shrimp out of the pot and showed us how to peel them. At first I didn't want to eat them, but I couldn't let Claude and Isadore do something that I wouldn't do. So I tried one. It was so tasty that I kept peeling and eating until I thought I would pop. I didn't touch any of the other delightful-smelling food the neighbors had brought.

Claude watched me as my pile of shrimp shells got higher and higher. "You think that's good. Wait until you taste river shrimp. We have box traps out in the river to catch them. You can swim out to help Jean Baptiste and me pull them in. They're even better than bayou shrimp." I didn't think that was possible.

32

Get-Togethers

In Acadie, we had always spent Saturday evenings with friends and neighbors enjoying music and dancing. After our vegetables were planted in Louisiana, we had frequent shrimp boils, and sometimes crab boils, with our neighbors.

The Acadian families who had lived in Louisiana long enough to build houses that were bigger than our hut, took turns having Saturday get-togethers for everyone. We pushed the furniture against the walls so there was room for dancing. The women brought food. Some of the men played music on their fiddles. Other people clapped, sang, and tapped their feet in time to the music.

Claude showed Isadore and me how to keep time to the music by hitting two sticks or two spoons together. Since everyone danced, even the youngest children, I did too. I was glad to have time to relax and get to know Jean Baptiste's and Claude's sisters. We laughed and enjoyed being together. It was good to have fun again.

The French and Acadian people in Louisiana were all Catholics. Soon after we arrived, Papa had asked, "Can we go to Mass on Sunday?"

"A priest visits once or twice a year," said M. Richard. "He says Mass, blesses marriages that have taken place since his last visit, and baptizes babies. The rest of the year, we gather at one of our houses on Sunday mornings. We pray together and sing hymns."

"Just as we did in Acadie," said Papa.

Because of our new friends, I began to enjoy life more, and sometimes, I was even happy to be living in this strange land.

33

A New House

At last! Another summer was nearly over. The weather was still hot and humid, but not quite as uncomfortable as it had been. Papa stood at the door of our hut, looking out over the fields. "We'll be ready to start building our house soon."

I thought I would burst with happiness. I couldn't stop smiling. We'd been in Louisiana for almost two years, and we'd soon have a real house to live in again. We had eaten vegetables from our own garden for almost a year. Our animals were big and healthy. We grew most of our own food, and the neighbors gave us beef or pork whenever they could.

When we were ready to start building, all of our friends came to help: the Richards, the Comeaus, the Martins, the Daigles, Mme Hébert and her children, Mme Boudrot, and the Acadian families who were already settled when we came to Louisiana.

M. Richard put his tools on the ground and looked at Papa. "We'll help you first because your maman and papa need a better house to live in. Your little hut can't be very comfortable for them. The younger people can wait. We'll try to have several houses finished before winter winds start blowing."

I watched the men and boys make a row of small poles standing on end, side by side. "This is the way we built our hut."

"Yes, but this time we'll make it bigger," said M. Richard. "And we'll put another row of poles very close to the first, then attach planks on the outside. That will make your walls nice and thick, so your house will be cool in summer and warm in winter. And we'll make a plank roof. You'll see—it will look like our house."

"We'll show you how to cover the cracks to keep out the cold air in winter," said M. Terriot, Jean Baptiste's father.

"We know how to do that," said Papa. "We covered the inside of our walls with mud in Acadie."

"What did you mix with the mud to make it strong?"

"Marsh grass."

"We don't have marsh grass here. We use Spanish ..."

"Spanish moss," I interrupted. "I'm sorry. I didn't mean to be rude, but you use it for everything else."

"You're right. We use Spanish moss, and sometimes we add powdered oyster shells to make the mud even stronger. We call it *bousillage*." (mud-wall)

When it was finished, our house was bigger and stronger than the hut; it had a fireplace and a few windows. Like the hut, it had a dirt floor, but it was big enough for beds for the adults and mattresses on the floor for the children. And what made Maman happiest, her loom and spinning wheel didn't have to be pushed against the wall when it was time for us to go to bed. Papa even extended the roof a little so Grand'maman and Grand-père could sit in their rocking chairs in the shade of the house right outside our front door.

We enjoyed relaxing outside in the evening after our work was finished. I liked to watch the stars begin to light up the sky, and to listen to crickets and night frogs sing their evening songs. We smelled sweet jasmine and honeysuckle, and waited for cool breezes.

Fireflies flitted around, their little blinking lights brightening the dark evening. Sometimes the younger children tried to catch them.

At night we kept our windows open to cool the house, but that made it easy for mosquitoes to come in, too. I was glad Mme Richard had showed Maman how to make mosquito nets to drape over our beds so the mosquitoes couldn't get to us. A few times, when I didn't put the net all the way around my bed, the little pests hummed and bit me all night. I soon learned to take the time to fix the net carefully.

Of course, after our house was built, we helped Mme Hébert, Mme Boudrot, the Martins, the Daigles, and the Comeaus build theirs.

We were always busy, but I didn't mind the work as much as I did during the hottest part of the summer. We finally had a house with room for the furniture Grand-père had built for us. Our fruit trees were healthy and would start bearing fruit soon. We were growing enough food for the family. I breathed a happy sigh whenever I looked around and thought about what we had accomplished. I looked forward to the time when our farm would supply enough for us to trade for more animals and anything else we needed.

34

Grand'maman

Everyone in the family looked healthier and happier every day—everyone but Grand'maman. She grew thinner, even with the vegetables from our garden and Maman's good cooking. By the time we moved into our new house, she spent most of her time in bed. It was hard for her to walk outside to her rocking chair, even though she seemed to enjoy sitting there with Grand-père during the day while he whittled, and with the rest of the family at the end of the day.

One evening when we came in from the fields, Maman told us that Grand'maman was much weaker. I held her hand and told her how much I loved her. After everyone finished eating, we gathered around her bed. She spoke to us in a whisper.

"I've had a good life. I have a good husband and loving children and grandchildren. You have made me happy. Leaving Acadie was the worst thing that ever happened to me. Coming here from Maryland was exhausting, but it was the right thing to do. I'm happy because I see how happy you are. Marguerite sings again. Everyone smiles and laughs. I can leave you, knowing you have a good life again. Please take care of Grand-père—he'll need all of you."

We took turns that night sitting next to Grand'maman's bed. She died during the night, holding Grand-père's hand. It had been too much for her frail body: being sent away from her home in Acadie, the long, hard trip on the ship to Maryland, almost eleven years in Maryland with too little to eat, and another difficult trip on the sailing ship to Louisiana.

We buried her the next day on our land. We put a wooden cross on her grave and built a little fence around it. I felt empty inside. My Grand'maman with the sweet smile was gone. I missed her very much, but I thanked God she had lived until we reached Louisiana. Now we could visit her grave and bring flowers to her. She would still seem close to us.

35

Another Difficult Decision

We were busy working in the fields when Isadore dashed past. "Come on. Hurry. A flatboat is on the river, and I think it stopped near M. Richard's house. Let's go see."

Papa, Michel, Jacques, and I dropped our hoes and ran past our house yelling, "Flatboat!" Grand-père leaned on a stick and limped along the path. Maman and the girls followed close behind.

Gasping for breath, with my lungs feeling as if they were going to burst, I caught up with Isadore. "This is the first time strangers have stopped on the river since we're here. I can't wait to hear about their adventures."

M. Richard was talking to the men when we arrived. "Where are you from?" he asked. "And where are you going?"

"We have rice farms upriver from here. We're on our way to New Orleans and will take any crops you want to sell."

We spent the afternoon listening to stories of their trips downriver. The men also talked about the trading ships that went back and forth from New Orleans to France.

"How will you get back to your farms?" I asked.

"We'll walk back because we can't row against the current on a flatboat. It's a long walk, but the people in New Orleans pay us well for the goods we have to sell. The farmers who live a few miles downriver in the settlement called the German Coast provide most of the food for the people of New Orleans. But they're always delighted to buy our rice."

"What will happen to your flatboat when you walk home?"

"We'll break it apart and sell the lumber before we leave New Orleans."

Isadore and I went back to M. Richard's house after supper to hear more of the men's stories. I could have listened all night. It was very late when I left, but the men were planning to leave early in the morning, and I knew they were tired. They spent the night in M. Richard's barn, and left as soon as the sun came up the next morning.

Since we left Acadie, I had seldom thought about my daydreams of being a ship's boy. It seemed so long ago that my cousin Jean and I sat under a tree in our apple orchard planning great adventures on sailing ships. Hearing the men talk about their trips had brought back all my yearning for adventure.

Why had my daydreams ended? Because I was so busy? Because Jean wasn't with me to make plans? Or was it because sailing had been a child's dream? I was too old to be a ship's boy, but I could be a sailor. The thought of adventure still made my heart beat faster. Could I find Jean? Did I want to sail without him? When he and his family left Acadie, I had promised him I would find him, and someday we would sail together.

An empty spot deep inside ached whenever I thought about Jean. Even though fourteen years had passed, I still missed him terribly. I wanted to see him again. I wanted to sail with him.

I had enjoyed the trip on the sailing ship from Maryland to Louisiana. That was a lot easier than cutting down trees, building houses, and planting and harvesting crops. If I became a sailor, I would get away from the awful heat and humidity in Louisiana and the exhausting work. I would get away from mosquitoes, snakes, and alligators. That thought made me smile. But I would have to leave my family, and I would miss them terribly. My smile went away.

What should I do? Should I go? Or should I stay? Papa once told me he was sorry he hadn't let me leave when I wanted to.

Maybe I could get a ride on a flatboat the next time one passed by on its way to New Orleans. Then I could get a job as a sailor on one of the sailing ships that arrived from France. Maybe I would find Jean. He might already be a sailor. Or he and his family might be living in France. We had heard that most of the Acadians who had escaped to Ile St. Jean had been captured and sent to France. These thoughts crowded my mind, and I couldn't think of anything else.

I decided to go for a walk one pleasant afternoon. I was tired of the constant knot in the pit of my stomach and the tightness in my throat. I had to make a decision, one way or the other, because I couldn't stand not knowing what I wanted to do.

Grand-père sat on a bench in front of the house, whittling. One tiny wooden animal stood next to him. He smiled at me when I passed.

Elizabeth was talking and laughing in the front yard with some of her friends—young ladies who would someday be good Acadian wives. Jean Baptiste was courting one of them. Was I ready to start courting?

Papa was in the fields, checking the crops and pulling weeds. He waved when he saw me. He had recently marked off a section of his land. "This will be yours," he said, "when you're ready to get married." Whenever we had a little extra time we chopped down a few trees, clearing the land for the house that I would build someday.

I walked to the little yard where Grand'maman was buried. The sweet smell of honeysuckle surrounded me. I sat on a fallen tree and said a prayer for her. Grand'maman had always been gentle and quiet, always happy as long as she was with her family. I missed her so much. Would I miss the rest of my family if I went away? Would they miss me?

On the way home, Isadore waved. "Come help me. I know how we can catch lots of shrimp, faster than Claude catches them." Isadore held up the net he was making. "We'll row a pirogue down the bayou with the net hooked on the back. Shrimp will get caught in it. I know it will work. If we catch lots of shrimp, we can dry them and send them to New Orleans when a flatboat stops here. The men will sell them for us. We'll save our money until we have enough to buy a few more pigs and another cow."

"That sounds like a good idea," I said. "We'll try it. I'd like to have more animals."

When I got close to our house, Maman was singing a happy tune. The smell of fresh cornbread and soup made me hungry.

I could go to faraway lands. I could see vast oceans, high snow-covered mountains, thick jungles, strange animals. I could eat food I'd never eaten before. I could meet lots of people. I could earn money. I could be a sailor. Is that what I wanted? I didn't know.

I thought of the many times someone in my family said how important it was to be with family.

Papa had said, "We will survive as long as we can stay together."

As we watched our houses in Grand Pré burn, Grand-père had said, "As bad as things are right now, at least we are together." Another time he said, "We'll be happy again if we are with our people."

Grand'maman had said, "Don't worry about me. I'm right where I want to be, with my family and friends."

I thought about how much help Papa needed. We were just getting started. It would be difficult for him to do all the farm work with just Michel and Jacques to help him. I thought about Maman, her smile and her happy songs. My younger brothers and sisters. My friend Isadore. My new best friends, Claude and Jean Baptiste. Antoine, who was happy and healthy again, and always had a big smile for me. He and Emilie often came to our house to visit my brothers and sisters. And Grand-père. How much longer would he live? How many more years would I have to spend with him?

I couldn't sleep, and I couldn't think of anything else. Nobody could make a decision for me. What should I do? Could I leave my family after all we had gone through together?

Papa once told me, "An Acadian boy doesn't run off on a sailing ship. He helps his family until he is old enough to get married. Then he builds his own house, and farms his land close to his family's home. He and his papa work together and help each other. That's the way of life for Acadians."

I was twenty-five years old. I would probably already be married if we hadn't been sent away from our home in Grand Pré. Now that we were settled in Louisiana, I could get married, build my own house, and continue to help Papa. We could plant more corn and raise more animals. Is that what I wanted to do?

Sailing might be exciting, but I'd miss my family as much as I missed Jean and Grand'maman. And I might never find Jean, even if I sailed. Our work was getting easier since we grew enough food for our family, and had already grown enough extra corn to trade for a cow and a calf.

I also had to think about the permanent house that Papa and I wanted to build. We often talked to our Acadian friends about the houses we had seen in New Orleans when we arrived from Maryland. We all hoped to build that kind of house soon. I knew I should help Papa with this. Grand-père probably wouldn't live too many more years, and a house with more windows to catch the cool breezes in the summer would make his life more comfortable. The house would be raised so we wouldn't worry about floods, and it would have a porch where Grand-père could sit in his rocking chair. There would also be more room downstairs because we planned to build a loft for the boys and me.

"Papa," I said a few days later, "You and Grand-père have been trying to tell me something for years, but I had to figure it out for myself. I have gone through so much with my family. I finally realize what is important. I am an Acadian. I am a farmer, not a sailor. I want to help you grow more crops and have a bigger, better farm. Soon I hope to get married and have a home and a farm of my own, close to yours. I want to continue to help you and Maman.

"Someday I'll go to New Orleans. And maybe someday I'll sail across the ocean. But for now, I'm here to stay. I'm home. I'm happy. I'm at peace—at last!"

Papa tried to answer me, but his voice broke. So he just hugged me.

Part Six
Epilogue: A Good Life
1769-85

Epilogue
A Good Life

A cadians continued to arrive in Louisiana from the American colonies until 1768 because they wanted to come to an area where many French people lived. Whenever we heard of the arrival of a new group, we all gathered to greet them with hugs and smiles. We were delighted to see friends and relatives again and to welcome Acadians we didn't know. We shed many tears for those who had died because of the harsh treatment they had been forced to endure for so many years.

I kept hoping Jean and his family would come to Louisiana. I still missed him and wished we could be together someday.

In 1785 a large group of Acadians arrived from France. When I heard that the first ship had landed in New Orleans, I did what I had told Papa I would do someday. I traveled downriver to New Orleans on a flatboat. I went to the large building where Acadians stayed until they received their land grants. I couldn't stop smiling when I found the Melanson family—friends from our church in Grand Pré. But my smile turned to a frown when I saw how thin and pale they were.

Claude Melanson appeared too exhausted to talk, but insisted on telling me his family's story. "We left Grand Pré a month before everyone was deported, by sneaking through the woods. The Micmacs helped us reach Ile St. Jean. They gave us food and a place to stay when we needed it. Life in Ile St. Jean was hard. We tried to grow crops but often had little to eat."

"Do you know anything about my cousin Jean and his family?" I asked. "They also left for Ile St. Jean a short time before we were deported."

"No, I heard nothing about them."

"Did you get any news of Acadie after we left?"

M. Melanson sighed. "Two months after the ships sailed from Grand Pré in 1755, Lieutenant-Governor Lawrence was named governor of Nova Scotia. His soldiers continued to search for and deport Acadians from Acadie. At the end of 1758, we, along with others who had fled to Ile St. Jean and Louisbourg, were captured and sent to France.

"Many families were given farmland, but the soil was too poor for us to grow enough vegetables to feed our families. My father, my brothers, and I tried farming in several different places where we were sent to live, but very little grew in the hard, rocky soil. We lived for twenty-six years on a few pennies a day the French government gave us."

My heart dropped. My family had suffered many hardships beginning thirty years ago, from the time men and boys were jailed in Grand Pré until we settled in Louisiana. We had worked until we were ready to drop, preparing the forestland for our farms and our homes. But we had been in Louisiana for sixteen years; we now lived in nice homes and our farms were prosperous. We had good lives and were happy. At the same time, many of our friends and relatives were still suffering—and we hadn't known what was happening to them.

"How did you get here?" I asked.

"Some of our Acadian friends received letters from families who settled in Louisiana. They said we would have a better life here, but we were too poor to pay for passage on a sailing ship. Then the Spanish ambassador in Louisiana went to the king of Spain and asked him to pay our expenses and bring us here. The ambassador told the king we are good farmers and willing workers."

M. Melanson smiled. "The king wanted more settlers in Louisiana to help protect the land from the English, so he agreed to pay for our trip and help us get started. Several more ships are being prepared to transport many more Acadians who want to come here."

From then on, whenever I heard that a ship carrying Acadians had arrived from France, I returned to New Orleans to greet the people. Many of our friends, relatives, and neighbors from Grand Pré were among the new arrivals. They told me about many others who had died, some while they lived in Ile St. Jean, some during the terrible trip to France, and others who tried to make a living in France. The weight on my shoulders felt a little heavier every time I talked to another Acadian family because no one knew where Jean and his family were. Maybe they had died, too. Maybe I would never see Jean again. I always returned home with a heavy heart.

One happy day I went back to New Orleans to meet another group that had arrived from France. My heart leapt to my throat as I recognized the first person I saw when I walked into the warehouse where they were staying. He looked older and thinner, but it was Jean! I couldn't believe I had found him after so many years. I thought I would burst with joy.

I grabbed my cousin and hugged him, not wanting to let him go. "Jean, is it really you? I have waited for this day for years."

Tears rolled down Jean's cheeks. "We didn't know what had happened to you. When we were sent to France, I didn't think we'd ever meet again. When I found out we would be allowed to come to Louisiana, I hoped you might be here. I have so much to tell you, and so many questions to ask. How is your family? Are you happy here?"

"Yes, life is good. And now that you're here, it will be as good as it was in Acadie."

I couldn't stop smiling—I couldn't stop looking at Jean. But I had to stop long enough to give thanks to God for bringing him and his family safely to Louisiana.

Jean and I didn't achieve our dream of sailing to France on a trading ship. Instead, I sailed up the Mississippi River from New Orleans with him when the Spanish officers accompanied the recently arrived Acadians to select their land. Jean and Oncle Jules were given land grants close enough to my home that we could visit often. We were together again at last, and nothing could have made me happier. Of course, my family and neighbors helped them get settled. We worked in our fields, worshipped God together on Sundays and holy days, and enjoyed life together—singing, dancing, and playing music.

Our children, and later our grandchildren, became best friends. My children and grandchildren taught Jean's children and grandchildren how to live like Louisiana Acadians.

Yes, we had a good life.

Afterword

This is a work of fiction, based on the history of the deportation of the Acadians from Nova Scotia between 1755 and 1759. Jacques Cartier, Lieutenant-Governor Charles Lawrence, Lieutenant-Colonel John Winslow, René Leblanc, François Landry, Joseph Landry, Louis Judice, and the Micmac Indians were real people. Their stories are factual, as is the story of what was done to the Acadians. The other people in the story are fictional, but the events are based on history.

Historians tell us there were about eighteen thousand Acadians in Nova Scotia in 1749. Thousands fled before *Le Grand Dérangement* (The Great Upheaval) in 1755. At the time of the deportation, between seven thousand and ten thousand Acadians lived in the areas of Port Royal (renamed Annapolis Royal by the English), Minas Basin (the area around Grand Pré), Fort Beauséjour (renamed Fort Cumberland), Fort Edward at Pisiquid, and surrounding areas. Many escaped into the woods and made their way to New Brunswick, Quebec, Ile St. Jean (now Prince Edward Island), or the fort at Louisbourg on Ile Royale. The Micmacs often gave food to the Acadians and helped them hide from the English as they tried to reach a safer place to live. The English soldiers continued to search for runaway Acadians until 1759.

Around the time the Acadians were imprisoned in Grand Pré, similar events were taking place in other parts of Nova Scotia where many Acadians lived. On August 10, 1755, four hundred men from the Chignecto and Chipoudy Bay areas were imprisoned at Fort Cumberland. They were told they would be deported to the French fortress at Louisbourg as soon as vessels arrived to transport them.

At the end of August, when ships arrived in Annapolis Royal to remove the Acadians from their homes, the men hid in the woods. However, the commander at Fort Anne (called Fort Royal by the Acadians) told others who had stayed behind that all would be allowed to return to their homes at the end of the war. Also, if they surrendered, they would be allowed to choose the English colony where they would live until the war ended. Many turned themselves in, but soon found out that nothing that they had been told was true.

On October 13, 1755, eight ships sailed from Chignecto Basin into the Bay of Fundy carrying nearly eighteen hundred Acadians. Accompanying them were three warships carrying twenty-one Acadian prisoners. The ships anchored near Annapolis Basin for two weeks waiting for the ships from Minas Basin. They were not going to Louisbourg as the people had been promised, but to the American colonies.

The five ships from Grand Pré were joined by five ships from Pisiquid and four more from surrounding villages. These fourteen ships sailed into Minas Basin on October 21 carrying more than twenty-six hundred Acadians from the Minas area. They sailed into the Bay of Fundy to travel with the eight ships from the Chignecto area that were awaiting them. On October 27, the twenty-two ships, accompanied by four warships, transported over four thousand Acadians from their homes and land.

On December 8, over sixteen hundred more Acadians on seven ships sailed from Annapolis Royal. They were escorted by one warship.

The Acadians were sent to the following American colonies: Virginia, Maryland, Pennsylvania, Massachusetts, South Carolina, New York, Georgia, and Connecticut. Thousands died as a result of the deportation, either on the ships or in the following winter months. There were smallpox epidemics on many of the ships. The governors and the people in the American colonies didn't want Acadians in their colonies any more than the Acadians wanted to be there. In some of the colonies, the authorities gave Acadians leaky ships to return to Nova Scotia. In others, the people collected money to send the Acadians back to Nova Scotia.

About twelve hundred Acadians who were transported to Virginia in 1755 were sent to England the following year by the governor and council of Virginia. They lived there until 1763, when they were sent to France.

Nearly four thousand Acadians escaped to New Brunswick. The British military patrolled the coasts and raided the Acadian settlements, making it impossible for the Acadians to fish or grow crops. Many died of starvation and sickness.

* * *

In July 1755, before the deportations began, Charles Lawrence wrote to the British authorities to tell them he planned to remove the Acadians from Nova Scotia. They neither approved nor tried to prevent his actions. Lawrence wrote again in October, informing the authorities that the Acadians had been dispersed. The following October, Lord Halifax of Great Britain wrote to Lawrence to commend him and to notify him that he had been named governor of Nova Scotia.

About six hundred Acadians left Halifax in November and December of 1764 for Saint Domingue (the island of Hispaniola).

They planned to travel from Saint Domingue to Louisiana, then to Illinois. Several hundred more left Halifax the following spring. Most of those who didn't die of sickness went to Louisiana and stayed there.

On July 26, 1758, the English captured the fort at Louisbourg on Ile Royale. Between three thousand and four thousand Acadians were transported to France. Over three thousand Acadians who were living in Ile St. Jean were also captured and sent to France. Less than half of the Ile St. Jean captives reached their destination. Close to one thousand drowned when three ships sank while crossing the Atlantic Ocean. Nearly eight hundred died of sickness while aboard the other ships on their way to France.

In 1762, France turned Louisiana over to Spain rather than lose the territory to England. When the Treaty of Paris was signed on February 10, 1763, France gave up its claims to land in North America, except for a few islands. All land in North America east of the Mississippi River belonged to England, with the exception of New Orleans and the land stretching west between the river and Lake Pontchartrain, Lake Maurepas, and Bayou Manchac. According to the treaty, Acadians who were being held in British territories were given eighteen months to move to French soil.

Some Acadians returned to Nova Scotia in 1763, but they were no longer landowners. They had to work on farms owned by English people, who, once again, needed the Acadians because the English didn't know how to care for the dikes. Many other Acadians went to Quebec. About four thousand traveled to Louisiana from the American colonies, from the jails in Halifax, and from the French West Indies.

The Spanish government wanted more colonists to settle in Louisiana. The king of Spain agreed to pay for ships to bring the Acadians living in France to Louisiana. Seven ships brought 1,596 Acadians to New Orleans between May and October 1785. The Spanish government gave them land grants, tools for farming, and enough food to survive until their first crops could be harvested. They settled in south Louisiana.

Most of the descendants of the 1755 Nova Scotia Acadians now live in Nova Scotia, New Brunswick, Quebec, Louisiana, New England, and France. Several hundred thousand descendants of the Nova Scotia Acadians now live in Louisiana, where they are called Cajuns.

In 2003, Queen Elizabeth II's Canadian representative issued a royal proclamation acknowledging the "tragic consequences" of the expulsion of the Acadians by the English, "including the deaths of many thousands of Acadians."

Chronology

1534—Jacques Cartier explored the St. Lawrence River and claimed this area of Canada for France.

1605—The first French settlers in the New World arrived in Port Royal, Acadie.

1607—The first English settlers in the New World arrived in Jamestown, Virginia.

1755—Acadians were deported to the American Colonies.

1758—Louisbourg was captured; Acadians there and in Ile St. Jean were sent to France.

1763—Treaty of Paris. Acadians were allowed to leave English-controlled lands.

1764—Acadians began to arrive in Louisiana.

1785—Nearly sixteen hundred Acadians who had been living in France since 1758 were brought to south Louisiana by the Spanish government.

Pronunciation Guide and Glossary

aboiteaux (ah bwah TOE)—Man-made ditches for carrying water, with a gate to adjust the flow so the water could drain from the land into Minas Basin and the Bay of Fundy. The gates, which opened only one way, would not allow the water to flow from the basin to the land.

Acadia—The English word for Acadie.

Acadie (ah CAH dee)—A French colony in eastern Canada in the 1500s to the 1700s. Today, the areas of Nova Scotia, New Brunswick, Prince Edward Island, and Newfoundland where French-speaking people live.

ange (ahnzh)—The French word for angel.

Arpent—An old French method of measuring land equaling about an acre.

Auguste (ah GOOST)

Boudrot (BOO dro)

Bousillage (BOO see ahzh)—A wall made of wood, mud, and moss

breeches—Men's pants that reached just below the knee.

Brigette (Bri ZHET)

Cajun (KAY jun)—The name for Acadians living in Louisiana. The word Acadian is pronounced *A KAH zhahn* in French. After the Acadians reached Louisiana, the first syllable was dropped. The local French pronunciation was *KAH zhehn* in the late 1700s and 1800s. The English pronunciation *KAY jun* is now used.

Charles (SHAR lez)

Comeau (CO mo)

Cornwallis, Edward—Governor of Nova Scotia from 1749 to 1752.

Daigle (daig)

dike—A mound of earth and rock built to hold back water.

frond—A leaf made up of several leaflets on the same stalk, such as a palm.

Gaspereau (gas per O) River—A river in Nova Scotia that flows into Minas Basin.

grand'maman (grahn mah MAH)—Grandmother.

grand-père (grahn PAIR)—Grandfather.

Grand Pré (grahn PRAY)—A village in Acadia. Grand Pré means "great meadow."

Hébert (A bair)

hold—The inside of a ship, below the deck, where goods are stored.

ile (ill)—The French word for island.

Ile St. Jean (ill saynt ZHAWN)—The island that is now called Prince Edward Island.

Jacques (zhahk)

Jacques Cartier (zhahk car TEE AY)—A French explorer who explored the St. Lawrence River and claimed the area for France in 1534.

Jean (zhawn)

Landry (LAHN dree)

Leblanc (leh BLAWN)

Louisbourg (LOO is burg)—A town on the northeastern tip of Acadia where a French fort was built. It was captured by the British in 1758.

Louisiane (LOO WEE zee ahn)—The French word for Louisiana.

M. (Muh SYUH)—Abbreviation for Monsieur, the French word for Mr.

Martin (mar TAN)

Mme (mah DAHM)—Abbreviation for Madame, the French word for Mrs.

maman (mah-MAH)—Mother.

Michel (me-SHELL)

Micmac, also spelled Micmaq or Mi'kmaq (MIHK mack)—A tribe of Indians in Nova Scotia at the time of the Acadians.

mosquito hawk—Another name for dragonfly, a flying insect with a long, slender body and two pairs of clear narrow wings.

mosquito net—A fine net used to cover beds to keep out mosquitoes.

Nova Scotia (NO vah SKO shah)—A province in southeastern Canada.

oncle (awnk)—Uncle.

palmetto—A type of small palm that has fan-shaped leaves.

papa (pah-PAH)—Father.

Pierre (pee-YAIR)

Saint Domingue—An island in the Caribbean Sea which is now called Hispaniola.

spruce beer—Beer made from the young shoots, the new growth, of spruce trees.

tante (tahnt)—Aunt.

Terriot (TAIR e o)

Thibodeau (TIH bo do)

weirs (wirz)—A method of catching fish by placing sticks in a stream to trap the fish.

Note: The sound of the letter *n* in the French words in this glossary (ange, Jean, maman, Martin, oncle, tante) is "open." The tongue does not touch the front teeth.

Bibliography

www.acadian-cajun.com

www.acadian-home.org

Ancelet, Barry Jean, Jay Edwards, and Glen Pitre. *Cajun Country.* Jackson, MS: University Press of Mississippi, 1991.

Arsenault, Bona. *History of the Acadians.* Ontario: Lemeac Press, 1978.

Brasseaux, Carl A., ed. *Quest for the Promised Land: Official Correspondence Relating to the First Acadian Migration to Louisiana, 1764–1769.* Translated by Emilio Fabian Garcia and Jacqueline K. Voorhies. Lafayette, LA: The Center for Louisiana Studies, University of Southwestern Louisiana, 1989.

_____. "Acadian Immigration into South Louisiana, 1764–1785." Online. www.acadianmemorial.org. Acadian Memorial Archive. Ensemble Encore: Together Again! Essays.

_____. *The Founding of New Acadia: The Beginnings of Acadian Life in Louisiana, 1765—1803.* Baton Rouge, LA: Louisiana State University Press, 1987.

_____. "Metamorphosis of Acadian Society in Late-Eighteenth-Century Louisiana." Online. www.acadianmemorial.org. Acadian Memorial Archive. Ensemble Encore: Together Again! Essays.

_____. *Scattered to the Wind. Dispersal and Wanderings of the Acadians, 1755–1809.* Lafayette, LA: University of Southwestern Louisiana, 1991.

Chevrier, Cecile. *Acadia, Sketches of a Journey.* Dieppe, Canada: La Societé National de l'Acadie, 1994.

Daigle, Pierre V. *Tears, Love and Laughter: The Story of the Acadians.* Church Point, LA: Acadian Publishing, 1972.

Doucet, Clive. *Notes from Exile on Being Acadian.* Toronto: McClelland and Stewart, 1999.

Faragher, John Mack. *A Great and Noble Scheme.* New York: W. W. Norton, 2005.

Folse, John D. *Encyclopedia of Cajun & Creole Cuisine.* Gonzales, LA: Chef John Folse and Company, 2005.

Hebert, Donald J. *Acadians in Exile.* Cecilia, LA: Hebert Publishing, 1980.

Johnston, A. J. B. *Endgame 1758.* Sydney, Nova Scotia: Cape Breton University Press, 2007.

LeBlanc, Dudley. *The Acadian Miracle.* Lafayette, LA: Evangeline Publishing, 1966.

_____. *The True Story of the Acadians*. Lafayette, LA: Evangeline Publishing, 1966.

Lockerby, Earle. *Deportation of the Prince Edward Island Acadians*. Halifax, Nova Scotia: Nimbus Publishing, 2008.

Rieder, Milton and Norma. *The Acadian Exiles in the American Colonies, 1755–1768*. Metairie, LA: Rieder, 1977.

Ross, Sally, and Alphonse Deveau. *The Acadians of Nova Scotia Past and Present*. Halifax: Nimbus Publishing, 1992.

Stacey, Truman. *Louisiana's French Heritage*. Lafayette, LA: Acadian House, 1990.

Sternberg, Mary Ann. *Along the River Road*. Baton Rouge, LA: Louisiana State University Press, 1996.

Tallant, Robert. *Evangeline and the Acadians*. Gretna, LA: Pelican Publishing, 2000.

Winzerling, Oscar W. *Acadian Odyssey*. Baton Rouge, LA: Louisiana State University Press, 1955.

Wood, Gregory A. *A Guide to the Acadians in Maryland in the Eighteenth and Nineteenth Centuries*. Baltimore: Gateway Press, 1995.

About the Author

Ollie Porche Voelker is a retired teacher and educational diagnostician whose interest in genealogy led her to write Home At Last. She is a descendant of several Acadian families who were deported from Nova Scotia. Ollie lives with her husband in Destrehan, Louisiana, a suburb of New Orleans.